CINDERELLA SRN

Despite her tender years, Student Nurse Kate Cameron is like a mother hen, forever worrying about her patients and her family. So it's a huge joke when her friends transform her into a *femme fatale* for the hospital's Christmas Ball. The joke backfires though, when Kate finds herself falling in love . . . But what chance is there of a fairy-tale ending when this Cinderella has chapped hands and an unflattering uniform, and Prince Charming turns out to be Luke Harvey, the new senior registrar?

ANNA RAMSAY

CINDERELLA SRN

Complete and Unabridged

LINFORD
Leicester

First published in Great Britain in 1985 by
Mills & Boon Limited
London

First Linford Edition
published 2014

A catalogue record for this book is available
from the British Library.

ISBN 978–1–4448–1901–4

Published by
F. A. Thorpe (Publishing)
Anstey, Leicestershire

Set by Words & Graphics Ltd.
Anstey, Leicestershire
Printed and bound in Great Britain by
T. J. International Ltd., Padstow, Cornwall

This book is printed on acid-free paper

1

Wrapping the wings of her navy cloak closely about her, Student Nurse Cameron pushed her way through the swing doors of the Accident and Emergency Department. She was off duty at last, and out of that hot busy atmosphere into a crisp cold night.

It was Christmas week and even a busy city hospital could not escape that ancient magic in the air. Frost sparkled like powdered diamonds underfoot and the darkness held none of its usual fears for the scurrying forms of the nursing staff.

There it hung, the boldest and brightest star in the heavens, the star Kate had always looked for since she was a small child. She paused for a moment, staring up eagerly, memories surging back to tug at her heartstrings, memories of Christmases long past when her mother was still alive and she herself just a carefree little girl . . .

Kate shook herself back to the present and hurried on to join the other shadowy figures, white-capped and heavy-cloaked, heading for the welcoming golden lights of the new nurses' home, completed that summer along with the building Kate had just left. Warm breath made smoky wisps in the chill air. But tired feet and aching limbs would soon be forgotten, for this was the night of nights — Stambridge Royal Hospital's annual Christmas Ball. More of a knees-up really, but it pleased the powers that be to make things sound grandiose.

Even though a third-year nurse and in her final year of registration, Kate had never been to this much talked about event. This year there was to be no escape.

'Of course you're coming. Every self-respecting nurse and medic in the place who's lucky enough to be off duty will be at the hop. Just forget home for once. That sister of yours must be old enough to help out by now. It's time you stopped playing Cinderella and missing out on all the fun.' Kate's best friend Joanna was never one to mince her words. A statuesque blonde, she modelled her image on Monroe — and her admirers were legion. On the face of it the two girls had little in common and the most opposite of looks. But they had been friends since day one in the training school and worked happily alongside each other on the wards.

Kate knew better than to waste time in vain protests. Let the whole thing be over and done with. Then she could rush off home early in the morning and get on with the useful work of getting the house ready for Dad and for Vicky. And yes, Vicky *was* quite capable of holding the fort till then.

Joanna knew better than to take that familiar gentle smile as meek complicity. Kate might look like the type of girl who was so quiet and fragile she would get pushed around a lot, but she was actually quite a strong-principled lass with firm ideas on what she would or wouldn't do — especially if someone's feelings might get hurt. That was one of the very good reasons why Jo liked her, a lot.

But at the same time it was Joanna's view that everyone ought to be living life to the full. And in her book that meant plenty of play to balance all the hard work. 'I may not be the most efficient nurse at Stambridge Royal,' she liked to say, tossing her bottle-blonde curls, 'but I love my work — nearly as much as I love doctors. And I've certainly sampled plenty of *those*!' It tickled her to see the look on Kate's expressive face when she came out with one of her more outrageous pronouncements. But just wait, one day she'd accept one of her admirers' proposals and become a staid and proper GP's wife. Or maybe even a consultant's!

'And you never know, Kate, Dr Right might be just around the corner for you

— if you only give him the chance.'

Kate, occupied in weaving her long dark hair into one thick plait ready for bed, had smiled to herself. Another of Joanna's flights of fancy. Doctors might be fine to work with, on a strictly professional basis. But Kate had little time for the casual love affairs that were so common to hospital life, no liking for the gossip that surrounded the goings-on between the nursing and the medical staff. That god-like aura some of them cultivated put her off. And a secret suspicion that such clever and confident men would find her tongue-tied and boring away from the safety of the wards.

Kate hadn't yet mentioned it to Joanna, for the relationship seemed at too delicate and tentative a stage, but she *was* getting rather fond of someone. Jo knew, of course, quite a lot about Kate's circumstances. That her off-duty time was taken up with rushing home to housekeep for her widowed clergyman father; that in spite of clever Vicky managing to win that scholarship to boarding school it had meant every penny Kate could spare to help out with fees. That Kate had been herself a happy-go-lucky teenager when her mother met with that tragic and pointless accident. But she did not yet know about Adrian.

He was, Kate supposed, a 'sort of' boyfriend at the moment. They had been brought together through a love of music. The 'sort of' was because nothing had been said or *happened* exactly between them. Just a few concerts, and that picnic lunch of course.

Kate played the piano very well and sometimes, when Adrian — who besides playing at her father's church taught at the local comprehensive — was otherwise occupied, Kate would take over his duties at the church organ. He had given her a few lessons on the necessary change of technique. 'Make your fingers hit the keys like little hammers,' he had advised. 'Put your hand over mine while I play, and feel how my fingers are working.'

Afraid that she must be blushing like some silly schoolgirl, and fearful that this calm and kindly young man might sense the tremor she could not control in her own fingers, Kate did as she was asked. Trying to concentrate on the technique rather than the intimacy of the moment, just the two of them up there in the organ-loft of the echoing empty church, Kate was heart-hammeringly aware of the sinewy warmth of his skin, of soft golden hairs on the backs of his hands which tickled her palms and sent this extraordinary feeling all the way down to the bottom of her spine. A feeling that was to haunt her in the quiet moments for days after; especially at night, alone, in her bed.

Either Adrian Horry was extremely chivalrous, or he was over-respectful of a vicar's daughter, but he behaved with such Victorian propriety that Kate began to think the first move — heart-sinkingly — must come from her! And looking back over that day of the picnic convinced her she was right. The admiration in his nice grey eyes spoke louder than words.

It had been a rare November day, remarkable for the warmth of the late autumn sun now low in a sky hazy with mauves, purple and gold. They had taken a picnic, at Adrian's suggestion, and driven out of the county to try the baroque organ of a famous church. Listening to the huge, glorious sound conjured up by her companion as it rolled around the beautiful old building, Kate had been both exhilarated and moved almost to tears. And later, watching those clever, magical hands so masterful on the car's steering-wheel, and the sensitive profile of their owner, Kate had a distinct feeling she might be falling in love.

They had discovered a sunny bank, spread a waterproof cover and a plaid woollen rug — as Adrian said, it did not do to take risks at that time of year — and sat down companionably to enjoy the thin November sun and eat their picnic. Wishing she had thought to bring a bottle of wine to provide a more romantic accompaniment to the food than coffee in a vacuum flask, Kate had pretended laziness and stretched out rather self-consciously beside Adrian, her arms clasped behind her head, her eyelids flickering with tension. He lowered his lean, tall frame to recline next to her, so close she could feel the warmth coming from him and the sound of his breathing . . .

After a few moments, disappointed that he made no move towards her, Kate surreptitiously opened her eyes. And closed them again quickly. He had propped himself on one elbow and was regarding her with an expression of hungry intensity, and Kate had the distinct feeling that if she had not retreated once more behind the safety of closed eyelids, pretending to have noticed nothing — if she had only stretched out a hand towards him — their relationship would have taken a dramatic turn.

Since that day they had had little opportunity to see each other, and none alone. The end of the autumn term kept Adrian busy, and Kate's off-duty did not coincide with a December week-end. So there was nothing really to report to Joanna, and now the night of the ball had raced up so quickly . . .

Once inside the nurses' home, Kate headed rapidly for the telephone booth to ring her father, fumbling in her uniform pocket for a ten-penny piece. Thank heaven, for once the booth was unoccupied. A rather querulous voice answered her call and Kate's ready smile turned anxious. 'Vicky, love, you're safely back!'

'Course I am, since you made such a thing about it. I was having the most super time at Lucinda's. Her brother had brought some amazing friends home from Oxford. Now, thanks to you, you mean old spoil-sport, I've had to come home early!'

Kate bit her lip. 'Oh, Vicky, I'm so sorry. It was just this once, something I couldn't get out of. But I'll make sure to get away good and early tomorrow. And tell you what, I'll pick up a Christmas tree on my way from the station and we'll get the decorations down from the attic and soon have the place looking like it should.'

But the cross little voice was not so easily placated. 'Well, it's certainly not very Christmassy here at the moment. I'm cold, Daddy's out . . . and, oh, Kate! Why couldn't you be here to look after me like always, and have things ready?' The whine turned into the sad note of a disappointed child and Kate's heart ached for her cold, lonely little sister. But as always she tried to look on the bright side and cheer the girl up.

'It was good of the Fox-Roberts to invite you home with Lucinda,' she enthused warmly, unwilling to end the conversation on a sour note. 'Perhaps we could invite Lucinda to come and stay with *you* next hols.'

There was a splutter of sarcasm at the other end of the line. 'Fat lot there

11

is to do here! Anyway, I was really enjoying myself at her place . . . '

'I must go, Vicky,' interrupted Kate with a quick look at the fob watch pinned inside her top pocket. Vicky could go on like this all night if given the chance. 'Be a good girl and have some supper ready for Daddy when he gets in from Evensong. Tell him I'll be home soon. Bye now, love.'

She replaced the receiver with a sigh. The 'good girl' bit rang patronisingly in her ears, but she had to face the fact that she was now more mother than sister. Almost seventeen, the younger girl had such brains, such looks; one day she would go to Oxford University, have a brilliant career and marry someone clever and worthy of her. That would more than make up for all the financial hardship — if making up were needed for sacrifices so readily made.

Voices interrupted her reverie and Kate turned to find Joanna and Roz at her elbow. 'Just got to shower and shampoo my hair,' she smiled in answer to their cries of greeting and urges to get a move on.

Jo's cap was awry, her tumbled blonde curls framing a distinctly pretty face, flushed now with eager anticipation. 'Can't wait to get cracking on you, Cinders. We're really going to slay 'em tonight, we three!' She squeezed her friend's thin shoulders, winked hugely at the gingery Roz, and shepherded them both upstairs at a rate of knots.

The feverish atmosphere was now getting to Kate, the first stirrings of nervous excitement. Once in the safety of her room up on the second floor, she threw her starched white cap across to the bed, unpinning a startlingly luxuriant mass of hair that looked as though it was impossible to fold into its former neat pleat. Making herself push all thoughts of grumpy little Vicky to the recesses of her mind, Kate began to admit that the evening might after all be fun. 'And if I can't get out of it, I might as well try to enjoy myself. And maybe Jo and Roz can make something out of me if I wear some make-up for a change.' She laughed aloud and turned on some pop music on her little transistor radio, shrugged on a towelling robe and hurried off to find a vacant bathroom.

Thirty minutes later when Roz put her head round Kate's door, she found her in bra and pants drying her long wet hair and surrounded by a litter of discarded clothes. Not at all like her usual neat and tidy self. Roz raised her almost non-existent eyebrows and grinned. 'What are you proposing to wear, Kate? Jo wants to know.'

'We-ell, I'm not exactly spoiled for choice.' Kate cheerfully indicated a cotton summer sundress, vaguely formal enough to pass for evening wear and carefully laundered and pressed.

Roz looked doubtful. 'Hmmm. What size are you? Ten. I'll see if I can come up with something a bit more . . . sexy.'

Kate's jaw dropped but Roz had already gone, leaving a rich aroma of perfume in her wake. Five minutes later she was back, clutching a make-up case, plastic cups and a bottle of sherry, 'To loosen us up a bit!'

Kate was bent almost double, still blow-drying the streaming mane of hair, now turning from seal black wetness to its true deep dark chestnut. She straightened up, massaging her aching back; those heavy tresses took such an age to dry. 'I don't know which is in worse shape tonight,' she remarked matter of factly. 'My back or my feet.'

Joanna charged in, dressing-gown clad, and collapsed on to Kate's narrow bed. 'Don't I know the feeling!' She examined her legs closely and the others followed suit, searching pallid bare legs for incipient varicosities. 'Please, God, bring me a dashing consultant specialising in varicose veins. Elastic stockings do nothing for my image. Just imagine it, the luxury of private treatment on your own kitchen table.' Jo proceeded to clothe her nether limbs in the sheerest of Dior tights.

'That's the trouble with the Nightin-gale ward system,' Roz pointed out seriously, at the same time busily darkening her eyebrows with deft strokes of pencil. 'We'd be better off working in one of those new hospitals where they've built the wards on the race-track layout. It saves so much legwork and it's much more efficient.'

But Kate was not having any of this. 'No running dear old Stambridge Royal down. At least, not tonight of all nights — season of goodwill and all that. Anyway, it's such fun on the old wards at Christmas.' She unplugged the hairdrier and began vigorously to attack her head with a bristle hairbrush. In spite of having little enough time for self-indulgence, the waist-length mass, rippling and shining with health, had never been cut short. It was one of her father's old-fashioned idiosyncrasies; like forbidding his daughters to wear jeans, whatever the fashion of the day.

Joanna drained the last drop of her sherry. 'Right, let's get to work, Roz.'

They settled their victim at the dressing-table, surveying the small pale face as if seeing it for the first time; noting huge dark eyes, a short straight nose and the appeal of the gently curving mouth. Features undistinguished in themselves but which can be the stuff models are made of. And skin fine and pale as best porcelain, soft and clear as a child's.

'Considering you do nothing to look after your complexion, Kate, it's downright unfair on the rest of us. I'm not going to bother with foundation — just a touch of peachy blusher to make your eyes sparkle. We want to keep that pale and interesting look, men really go for that. And for goodness' sake, Cinderella, sit still or you'll have mascara all down your nose!'

'Listen,' warned Roz, 'you're not roping me in to play the Ugly Sister — I intend to slay 'em tonight . . . that's if I can hide these hateful freckles!'

'You're silly to cover them up,'

advised the expert Joanna. 'Freckles are actually very attractive. Try some of my silver shadow on your eyes — you'll look stunning.'

She turned her attention back to Kate who was waiting obediently, eyes closed.

'There, Kate, what do you think of yourself now?'

Kate stared at herself dumb-struck. This was going to take some getting used to; white skin, darkly glittering eyes made even more emphatic by Joanna's skilful use of kohl; a full, rose-red mouth which had lost its soft innocence and gained a glistening, sultry pout . . . She had never even dreamed of looks so glamorous they could turn her insides to jelly. The looks of a total stranger — which could take some acting up to if you were in reality just an ordinary twenty-year-old with little experience of the blandishments of men.

'Th-thanks, Jo!' she stuttered, bewildered, not knowing whether she felt thrilled or scared. As though her whole body, not just her face, was unfamiliar, she moved on cotton-wool legs to where her simple frock hung limply on its hanger.

But Roz got there first. 'Whoa there, that won't match up to Cinders' new image.' She laid a gently restraining hand on her friend's narrow shoulder. 'Just a mo', love, Jo and I have something else in mind.' As she disappeared in a flurry of talcum, Kate reached out wistful fingers to stroke the comfortingly familiar fabric. Was it to be goodbye, then, to her old way of life? Some sixth sense warned that changes lay afoot, that something scary but inviting loomed ahead.

Roz was soon back, displaying a black velvet creation, strapless and form-fitting, as un-Katelike as the hapless victim could imagine.

Suddenly she panicked. I shouldn't be going along with this frivolity! What about all that shopping and cooking . . . and poor Vicky moping round an empty vicarage on her own? And I've never worn anything so — so *bare* in all my life. Nor want to start now! she thought frantically.

But such was her friends' determination that three minutes later Kate was ready, all but the shoes. Black satin would be ideal . . . but where to find some at this late minute to fit such narrow, slender feet?

'Forget the glass slippers, these'll do nicely.' In a last-ditch attempt to suppress her qualms under a show of nonchalance, Kate stuck her feet into the clumpy black lace-up shoes she wore on the wards. She traipsed comically about, reducing her companions to gales of affectionate laughter. The dress fitted like a glove; the shoes were pure comedy. Again Roz zoomed off on the scrounge.

Finally they surveyed each other critically, Kate wobbling uncertainly on spindly silver heels held on by a cobweb of frail straps. 'Not sure I can even get downstairs in these,' she muttered hopefully. Her lips felt tacky under their bright layer of gloss, her lashes stiff with mascara. The palms of her hands were decidedly clammy.

Roz was an apricot-headed siren in ice-blue satin, Joanna a vision ripe with promise in slithery buttercream silk. 'A ravishing trio 'n all,' was the breathless verdict of an Irish houseman, flying through the corridors to answer some life and death call. His admiration was not lost on Kate. Cinderella for the night, she felt a surge of adrenalin and determined to make the most of the experience. Let the sensible Nurse Cameron save her better self for tomorrow; the world would not miss her for just one night.

'Three little nightingales,' crowed Joanna, 'disguised as birds of paradise and waiting for a few larks!' They giggled inordinately at such wit, trooping down endless corridors to the scene of the ball. Jo gave Kate's arm a reassuring squeeze. For over two years now they had been close friends, but never before had she been successful in persuading the quiet, gentle Kate to join in the fun. And it wasn't that vicars' daughters lived on some higher plane than the rest. Kate just had a bit of a hard life one way or another. She deserved a night of fun.

By some miraculous means the hospital dining-room had transformed itself into a glowing cavern. Full of atmosphere, romantic dimly-lit spaces contrasted with hypnotically moving spotlights casting pools of rainbow light over the dance floor. Candlelit tables were glowing oases in the enticing gloom. Already the place was electric with heady excitement, vibrant with the pulsing beat of the band.

'Good grief,' enthused Roz, impressed by the scene that met their eyes. 'Some-one's put in some hard work here. Who'd have thought the old staff dining-room could look like this? Egg and chips'll never taste the same again! It's like an Aladdin's cave. Here, there's my man of the moment with your Tom, Joanna.

Come on, Kate, they're dying to meet you.'

Kate soon found herself caught up in a chattering crowd, sipping drinks and exchanging banter. The gin and tonic pressed upon her had a strange, bitter taste, but its effect on her tenseness was nothing short of wondrous. One more of these, thought Kate, and I'll be ready for anything. She peered less shyly over the edge of her almost empty glass, unaware that Joanna had warned Tom to make Kate's a double to help get her in the mood. At that moment a ripple of sudden interest ran through the little cluster of girls with whom she stood.

Five pairs of eyes, ranging from nervous to bold, registered the purposeful approach of a total stranger who threaded his way across the crowded dance floor, breasting the tide of dancers to steal, so it seemed, one from their midst. At the approach of this figure, moving easily through patches of light and shadow, almost menacing in his unusual height, Kate's shaky confidence crumbled.

I feel ridiculous, she thought wildly. Too tall and too skinny in this awful dress. It must have cost a bomb and it'll give people who don't know me entirely the wrong impression. Embarrassed by the nakedness of her shoulders and the curve of her breasts above the low-cut black velvet, Kate tried to shrink unnoticed to the back of the group.

The stranger halted before them. Kate longed to flee but swayed, rooted to the spot. This man could never look twice at her.

'Whoever is he?' someone muttered.

'He's gorgeous!' breathed another voice faintly.

Even the discreet lighting could not hide the glow of an unseasonal tan, diminish his athletic build, disguise that commanding air of authority. No junior doctor this, was the silent consensus. No work-worn, badly nourished house-man. This stranger, with his handsome head of close, rough-textured curls, bleached by some foreign sun to the same bronzed hue of his skin; heavy-lidded lazy eyes, returning their unabashed scrutiny with a cool, amused stare. Well aware of his own attraction, thought Kate with uncharacteristic resentment. In spite of his immaculate evening dress he looked an outdoor type, hard-living, used to taking his pick among women. Where on earth could such a man have sprung from? And what was his purpose at Stambridge Staff Ball?

His appetite for the fairer sex could be measured by the way he was giving them all a most unapologetic once-over. Kate shrank further into the background, her heart hammering with trepidation. Please Fate, have a more gentle Prince Charming in store for me tonight, she wished fervently, closing her eyes until the man had made his choice and moved away.

No one had spoken for the last thirty seconds. It seemed to Kate interminable — unbearable. Who would be his prey? She opened her eyes and looked straight into his.

'Come.' His voice was low and confident. A warm hand reached for hers, brushing lightly the smooth skin of her arm. An Englishman after all, Kate realised with a small start of surprise. And of all people he had chosen her! It must be that beanpole height which made her stand out in a group of pretty nurses, all far more eager than she for such a partner. As she stepped forward, mesmerised, an audible sigh ran round the others. Fancy Kate being the lucky one; but she really did look great tonight. What a dark horse she'd been! And as for that intriguing stranger, where *had* he sprung from with his tropical tan?

Fingering the tiny silver locket at her throat, the only outward indication of her inner turmoil, Kate struggled to play it cool, her small hand lost within his. A slight smile softened one corner of his hard mouth, feeling against his fingers the roughened skin of a surprisingly icy palm. This nymph might look like a princess but she earned her living the hard way. One of the nursing staff without a doubt; he was very familiar with the species.

One thing puzzled Luke. As they moved on to the dance floor it was obvious that his partner was attracting quite some attention. If female eyes lingered curiously on him, that was only to be expected, a stranger in their midst. But men's eyes surveyed the tall girl with blatant admiration mingled with what could only be described as surprised recognition. How come she was unpartnered, hadn't been snapped up before?

Curious. Curious indeed. And there was something else. For all she looked so composed, there was an endearing little tremor at the side of that very kissable mouth, a nervous trace of moisture in that chilly little palm. Yet the appearance was that of a sophisti-cated woman, well-versed in the art of pointing up her own beauty, of choosing clothes to flatter and accentu-ate every lovely curve of her young body.

Luke determined to read the truth in

her eyes, when he might succeed in trapping them with his own direct gaze.

Around them couples were doing their own thing to the strains of a rather outmoded foxtrot, some swooping rhythmically to the music, others attempting a wilder form of disco-dance. Others clinched amorously, barely moving on the same spot. Glancing hesitantly at her escort, Kate wondered what he had in mind, hoping her parish hall hop technique was not going to let her down.

Disdaining the thickest of the crush, the man led her to a quieter spot, one arm firmly bringing that tense young body right up against his own, a warm dry hand enveloping hers as closely and comfortably as a glove. Kate felt unreal, as though she were dreaming it all. Her heart thundered away against his jacket and she prayed he couldn't tell. She was just tall enough — with the help of those silver heels — to see over his shoulder. That was one thing to be grateful for, a partner who wasn't dismayed by the height those three-inch heels jacked her up to! Why, he must be six foot three easily.

How, for heaven's sake, did one foxtrot? Wasn't that the thing where Miss Dufty had said you mustn't bring your feet together? Kate chewed her bottom lip, unwilling to voice her lack of expertise. She must try at least to live up to his obvious expectations of her: Cinderella — Jo and Roz's joke! — for the night.

Prince Charming had said nothing beyond that one peremptory, 'Come.' His arm held her close, firm and supportive, his hard body guiding her steps with an intimate confidence that left Kate breathless and made her heart leap. It really didn't matter that she was no dancer. He led so easily they might have been partners for years. And high as those wretched heels might be, the top of Kate's head came only to the level of that stern, sun-bronzed jaw.

I'm actually enjoying myself, Kate shivered with delight. It's only for just this once, I'll work twice as hard tomorrow. But I never dreamed I could feel so . . . well, delicious. I feel pretty, actually pretty. And people are looking at me as if they're not sure who I am tonight. And they're looking at *him* too. Dare I ask his name? He hasn't asked mine. Think I'd better wait and see if he asks me to dance twice . . .

She smiled blissfully, aware of Jo and Roz's grins as they passed on the dance floor. It was amazing how well she and this man fitted together, like two spoons in a drawer. How silly to have been so nervous, scared even. Who could have imagined it would be such a thrill to be held closely in a stranger's arms. Would it feel as good with Adrian?

Still he didn't speak. From time to time Kate was conscious of him staring down at her, a curious searching gaze. She avoided his eyes, sensing they might find mirrored in her own all these unfamiliar, indescribable pleasures taking hold of her emotions. Once he intercepted a glance between Kate and a stunning blonde girl, was just in time to catch the shy proud grin that transformed her solemn expression. He smiled in secret amusement; all was most definitely not what it seemed.

Luke swung his partner in an extravagant twirl, enjoying the feel of that luxuriant mass of hair as it billowed out across his arm. Against his black evening jacket and the sultry black velvet of her dress, the girl's skin glowed like finest porcelain. He resisted with difficulty the longing to press his face against that smooth, flawless complexion. Something warned him that in spite of all she appeared, it would be only too easy to scare away his enchanting companion. Instinctively her thumb curled more closely about his, her cheek nestled against the shoulder of his jacket.

Then suddenly everything came to a halt.

He was standing back from her with a polite murmur of thanks, escorting Kate to a seat where he left her with nothing further than the politest of nods. Bewildered, she sat there alone for a few moments with her thoughts. Dance after dance had passed unnoticed; then out of the blue he had abandoned her. Just like that. How silly she had been; *was* being. Kate pulled herself together and went in search of Joanna.

'Who is he? What did he say? Where's he gone?'

Kate shrugged, trying to pretend it was of no consequence. 'I don't know the first thing about him. Is that the buffet starting? I'm famished.' And surprisingly she was. It was difficult not to succumb to the temptation to scour the room with eager eyes, but she found to her surprise that sudden fame had come upon her. Whether it was the effect of her new image, or simply the fact that her being there was unusual enough, Kate was instantly surrounded by admirers vying with each other to fill her glass or pile her plate with smoked salmon.

And most extraordinary of all was

her own performance, as she stood there flirting easily and elegantly with the most awesome of the medical staff. Can this really be me? Kate was quite astonished to find herself coolly handling the blandishments of a young obstetrician who obviously couldn't believe his luck in being granted the sight of a shy young nurse he remembered from his work on Gynae, displaying assets any girl would be proud of.

'And what plans have you for tomorrow night, did you say?' he persisted. A knowingly seductive finger began to tease her shoulder, leaving Kate with a strong desire to put the distance of the room between them.

'I'm off duty and going home,' she told him firmly. 'Excuse me, Ian. There's someone I must see.'

In the powder room Kate dabbed inexpertly at her mouth. The cherry-red gloss made her lips look unusually full and pouting. Were they really like that all the time, so generous and appealing?

How the wine made her eyes glitter and sparkle, as though with unshed tears. Confidence out of a bottle, she told herself severely; beauty out of a tube of cheap wax.

Joanna came in. 'Oh, there you are! We wondered where you'd slipped off to.'

'Escaping Ian Page's unwelcome attentions. I'm having a great time, truly, Jo. But it's not me, is it? I mean ... ' Kate indicated her finery with a dubious hand.

Jo gave her friend a strange look. 'Couldn't this be the real you? We all change as we get older — discover new things about ourselves. Maybe you've just been denying your true self,' she added darkly, accompanying her words with a reproving wag of the finger. Kate had to laugh and they emerged from the ladies' room like partners in crime, giggling together over their latest exploit. You really couldn't be serious with Joanna around.

Kate had almost, but not quite,

forgotten her mysterious partner, when he materialised out of the gloom once more at her side. This time they danced facing each other, a few feet apart. It gave him the opportunity to watch her closely and Kate felt hypnotised under his appraisal. The man had natural rhythm and a rather endearing unself-consciousness in spite of his aloof quality. Still he didn't speak and, taking her cue from this, neither did Kate. In some strange way it added to the magic quality of this evening, as though he really might be some enchanted prince from another world. It lent the experience a curious excitement to have so attractive a man apparently inter-ested only in her, seeking to dance with no one else, moving his body with supple ease to the heavy, insistent beat of a jazz-rock number. And *still* never choosing to speak.

In a half-light pierced with flashes and whirls of strobe, the medical world cavorted in an abandonment born of temporary escape from the harsh realities and stresses of hospital life. So where did he fit into all this, the sun-tanned figure now discarding his jacket, loosening a black bow tie and opening the neck of his dress shirt as the night grew ever hotter, the atmosphere more lunatic.

By now Kate had lost track of time as she swayed before him, shoulders gleaming like pearl above the strapless black velvet, the mass of her raven hair cascading in a rich dark waterfall, rippling down her back. As she danced, the side slit in her skirt parted to reveal her long slender legs and the flashing silver sandals.

Then, when the tempo changed and the last waltz was announced over the crackling microphone, instead of disappearing into the throng as mysteriously as he had arrived, the silent stranger remained standing there, looking deep into the very heart of her with those lazy cobra eyes. Transfixed, Kate moved helplessly towards him, her own eyes melting into his, her arms reaching out with a will of their own to clasp behind his neck.

What am I doing? Kate asked her conscience, aghast. This can't be me, ordinary Kate Cameron? But how can I let him know? We're both of us under some hypnotic spell neither of us wants to break with words. But for all I know he may be a married man with children — for he's a good deal older than I am.

A shiver of horror ran through her and, mistaking the brief tremor, the man's grasp tightened possessively about the slender, pliant body. All around them other couples moved sensuously, close in harmony and physical awareness. So when the lights dimmed to a faint glow and their lips blindly sought each other out, Kate was caught up in a surge of wild new emotions, finding herself being thoroughly, expertly and most dangerously kissed by a complete stranger.

When the lights came up and that sensitive, exploratory mouth broke into a triumphant grin, Kate was riven with mortification to hear the low farewell delivered in mocking Queen's English.

'Goodnight then, beanpole. You *were* in luck — finding a man to match!' And with a flash of excellent teeth in his lean brown face, he was gone.

2

'I'm home!'

Kate dumped her parcels in the echoing hallway and propped the best Christmas tree she had been able to get hold of so late in the week against the wall. In the distance a door slammed and Vicky appeared at the head of an elegantly curving staircase — which had seen better days, judging by the faded expanse of its threadbare carpet.

Instead of running down to greet her, Vicky leaned nonchalantly over the banister rail. 'So,' she observed aloofly, 'you've deigned to come home at last.'

Kate peered up at her sister, who was only visible from the waist up. Well, she was out of bed by midday so that was something to be thankful for.

'Come on down and lend a hand,' she encouraged. 'I've done some shopping on the way, so we can get cracking on the food. Come on or we'll never be ready for Christmas! Oh lor', Vicky, what on earth . . . ?'

The younger girl was swanking down the stairs, her lower limbs encased in skin-tight denim jeans.

'Dad'll have a fit!' said Kate faintly. 'You know he doesn't let us wear trousers. He *hates* them on women.'

A defiant Vicky tossed her sweeping blonde pony-tail like an arrogant young filly. 'Daddy knows. And he doesn't mind, so there. What's more, he says I can cut my hair off if I really want to.'

Shaking a disbelieving head, Kate headed down the maze of passages, Vicky trailing after her, watching idly as Kate unwrapped packages at speed and bustled around the large old-fashioned kitchen. With its Rayburn stove flanked by a rocking-chair and a wheel-back wooden carver loaded with comfy cushions, it was the only really warm place in the rambling wintry vicarage and people tended to gravitate there for comfort.

'Don't you like them?' Vicky smoothed the fabric sensuously over her slim hips. 'You can try them on. Lucinda's getting hefty and she can't stand the sight of herself in stretch jeans so she gave them to me. I didn't waste money on them, if that's what's biting you.'

'Okay, some time when I have a minute I might see how I look.' The words were out before Kate had really thought what she was saying, surprising her sister as much as herself, judging by the expression on the younger girl's face. So why am I all of a sudden interested in what I might look like in — well, uncharacteristic clothes! After-effects of last night? No, determined Kate, last night is best forgotten.

Vicky peered at her curiously. 'What's that on your eyes, Katie? Have you been wearing mascara? You haven't got it off properly, you know.'

Reaching in a drawer, Kate pulled out a cracked shaving mirror and peered at herself. She'd thought soap and water would remove all the traces of Joanna's artistry. Bother.

'You of all people,' said Vicky meaningfully. 'Wearing make-up and trying on jeans! Whatever's happening to my big sister? I know,' she sprawled in the wheel-back chair, feet balanced on the chrome rail of the stove, 'you've found yourself a man. Some macho consultant's made a pass at you and you've written off soppy old Adrian.' Her blue eyes grew wider as the fantasy went on, and Kate couldn't help but laugh.

'I suppose it's your imagination that makes you so brainy, my love. But I really don't know where you get your ideas about nursing life. Now come on, get your bottom off that chair and start doing something constructive.' Kate got out a jar of mincemeat, fetched fat and flour from the pantry and began to make pastry for the mince pies. There were a hundred and one jobs waiting to be done. As soon as these were in the oven she and Vicky could set to and strip the beds, get the twin-tub set up and all the accumulated washing — Vicky wouldn't have thought to do her clothes from school — under way.

With one of her sudden changes of mood, Vicky chattered on, her interest in Kate's love-life apparently forgotten. 'I'm thinking of going really short — it's all the rage. It takes me half an hour just to dry my hair and it's such a bore. Here, give me that spoon and I'll put in the mincemeat for you . . . Why don't you get your hair chopped off too?'

Kate grinned to herself as she lightly rolled out the pastry dough, stamping out each tartlet with quick, deft movements. Vicky in full flow didn't really wait for answers, she was far too wrapped up in her own life to be greatly interested in mousey old Kate. Just so long as mousey Kate was there to look after her and run round her when required!

'Where did you say Dad has gone?'

'Oh, visiting some new family who've moved into the parish,' came the disinterested reply. 'He said he wouldn't be late for lunch, but you know what he is.'

'I know,' smiled Kate fondly. As he cycled round the streets he'd be waylaid a dozen times by people seeking help, advice or just wanting a friendly word. She popped two dozen mince pies into the depths of the oven and ran her floury hands under the cold tap.

'Before we do the beds Vic, have a look at Dad's Christmas present. It's a bit extravagant and I know he loves his stone hot water bottle, but this will do his rheumatism a power of good.' She unpacked an electric blanket, found a screwdriver in a drawer and wired up an electric plug with easy skill. 'There,' she announced with satisfaction, 'now I can wrap that and put it under the tree.'

The quixotic Vicky now lapsed into sudden depression, watching her sister's useful hands. She would never be able to run a home, look after a family, cope with all the things that came so easily to Kate. She said so, miserably.

Kate hugged her warmly. 'Just wait ten years and you'll feel differently.

How many sixteen-year-olds have to do this kind of thing anyway? If things had been different, if Mum were still here, I wouldn't have had to learn to take her place. And you know, Vicky, we're so proud of all the things you *can* do well, all that Latin and History and so on. One day you'll go to Cambridge or Oxford and who knows what you may become? Just think of the exciting future that lies ahead.'

Her embrace was warmly returned by the lovable Vicky concealed beneath the pseudo-sophisticated veneer. 'I *am* glad you're back now, Kate. It's like Mum being here again — you even sound like her sometimes. Just to show I mean it, I'm going to make you a cup of tea.'

By the time the Reverend Cameron had wheeled his cycle up the drive, lunch was ready and waiting. 'What a welcome,' he rubbed his frozen hands with pleasure, 'to find my two beautiful daughters home and such a wonderful smell of cooking. Vicky, I must help you find those tree decorations this after-noon.'

After hugs and kisses all round he sniffed the air appreciatively, gladdened by the prospect of a good hot meal once again in his own kitchen. The parishioners were so very kind when Kate was away at work. No one would see their vicar go without a decent Sunday lunch, or a cooked supper on a freezing night. But when Kate was home — ah! Then it was almost like the old days.

'Did I ever tell you how like your beautiful mother you're getting?' he asked, catching gratefully at her hand as Kate transferred dishes to the big wooden table, its surface bleached pale with scrubbing.

'Frequently, Daddy,' came the calm reply as Kate bustled round the room like a young mother hen. Looking at the three of them, and at the photo on the dresser of a serene-faced, dark-haired woman smiling out at them all, heredity could clearly be seen at work. The tall spare father, still handsome in his fifties with that thick greying hair, the slight stoop of his bony shoulders as though the cares of the world often pressed heavily; and his two tall daughters with their slender upright frames, their graceful long necks and elegant limbs.

After the meal Michael Cameron sat awhile with his coffee, enjoying the warmth of the stove, the sight of his daughters chattering happily together over the washing-up. No man, the thought came to his mind, could ever be deserving of such girls; their worth was far above pearls. Vicky with her strong personality and fine young brain. Kate with her goodness and that beauty of face which mirrored the beauty within. So capable, despite the apparent fragility of her slender form.

Michael, himself a man without a selfish bone in his body, often worried over what Kate might be giving up to come home so frequently. But she would never be deterred, never allow him to cope for long alone. The time was coming when she must be encouraged to spread her wings; once fully qualified who knew where her future might lie? Certainly not here, with an ageing parent for company. Of course, that young organist was getting rather fond . . . but somehow Michael wished his daughter might meet a man of greater character. That was unfair, he chided himself. Adrian was a fine young man and if he was Kate's choice then so be it. At least she would stay near to her father.

Michael Cameron yawned deeply, the heat making him tired. He had been up since five-thirty to prepare for the early service which gave people the chance to attend before work. There was a faithful band of regulars, Kate being one of them when she was home. Vicky rarely came. He and Julia had never forced their daughters to go to church, ever conscious that it wasn't an enviable life being vicarage children.

'What's all this then, Dad?' Teasingly Kate indicated her sister's jeans. 'If I'd dared go out like that at Vicky's age you'd have put your foot down with a firm hand!' She perched on the edge of the rocking-chair, cuddling a steaming mug in her chapped red hands.

With a defiant glare, Vicky wrapped an arm about her father's neck, rubbing a rosy young cheek against his greyish pallor. He shook his head in rueful amusement.

'We-ll,' he admitted. 'I must try and keep up with the times. Mrs Rayner tells me all the youngsters wear them nowadays, and though I don't think jeans are at all pretty, who am I to be the arbiter of fashion?'

'And long hair's right out now, Daddy!'

Kate rolled her eyes dramatically. 'The gospel according to Vicky, heaven help us. She's obviously been using her fatal charm to effect on Mrs Rayner too — whoever *she* may be.'

'Ah now, Alice is new to the parish ... a wonderful person.' For some minutes the vicar enthused over the admirable qualities of this unfortunate lady who, widowed in her late thirties, had nevertheless struggled to raise three excellent and hulking sons, all away at boarding schools on army scholarships. Mrs Rayner, Alice, it appeared, had been extending her hospitality to Michael Cameron and was already proving herself an invaluable parish worker. 'There's nothing she won't tackle, from the PCC to playing the organ if Adrian's unavailable. We could do with more like Alice, yes indeed. Was that the front door?'

Feeling faintly resentful of the wondrous Alice, Kate jumped to her feet. 'I'll go — you have your rest.' She untied her pinny, shivering as she went out into the chill air of the unheated passages. Her cheeks were flushed from the heat of the oven, wisps of hair escaping from the loose chignon resting on the nape of her neck. She hoped it wasn't the Bishop or anyone important. You never knew who might come knocking on a vicarage door.

For one extraordinary moment the events of the previous night leaped unbidden to Kate's mind. So tired, she had slept the sleep of the dead. Awake, there'd not been a minute to think again of him. But just supposing Prince Charming had brought the silver sandal and come to claim his bride . . .

What rubbish, Kate Cameron. What on earth has come over you, letting Roz's jokey words plunge you into the realms of idle fantasy! Just put that man out of your head — you're bound to have to face endless post-mortems when you get back to the nurses' home. Idle speculations about a passing stranger who'll never cross your path again . . .

Kate gripped the big brass handle and swung the front door aside with such vigour that the figure on the other side instinctively retreated down the step, certain that he had arrived at an inconvenient moment.

They stared at each other in astonishment, she because her mind's eye had been full of another image; he because Kate glowed with such vitality he was stunned by the sheer physical attraction of her — even with a shiny nose and flour on her left cheek.

Sudden shyness gripped them both. It was always the way, for their relationship was starved of continuity. Each time she saw Adrian it felt to Kate as though she had to get to know him all over again, break the ice of their mutual shyness. How ridiculous! One of them must learn to behave like a mature adult with *some* social skills.

She broke into a peal of spontaneous laughter, so infectious that the tension immediately splintered. 'Oh, Adrian, how good to see you. I thought it might be the Bishop — and me looking like the wreck of the Hesperus.' Kate held the door wide in welcome. 'Come on in. You're just in time for coffee. Father and Vicky are in the kitchen.'

Emboldened by the ease of Kate's manner and the warmth of her greeting, the lanky young man stepped across the threshold, planting a clumsy peck on her warm soft cheek and thrusting a flat package into her hands. 'It's you I've come to see really, Kate. Just wanted to say 'Happy Christmas' and be on my way. You must be dreadfully busy.' He stood there, ill at ease in spite of Kate's welcome, fiddling with the knot of his neat college tie, his lean frame bulked out by the heavy sheepskin jacket. The lobes of his ears glowed red with the cold.

'I'm never too busy to see you, Adrian,' insisted Kate with more kindness than honesty. If only he would stop treating her like a piece of Dresden china, drop some of this dreadful over-respect for the vicar's daughter. It made her clam up inside, stifled her natural reactions for fear of disappointing him with the ordinariness of her real self.

'Leave your things in the hall and come and join us by the kitchen stove. It's so sweet of you to bring me a present — I'm afraid I haven't got round to wrapping yours yet. May I open this now or shall it go under the tree for Christmas Day?'

Chattering gaily, she drew him after her, down the quarry-tiled passages to the kitchen door.

Later, when he had gone, Vicky picked up Adrian's present — a book of organ music — and stared at it with disgust.

'Bach's Schübler Chorale Preludes. How *boring*.'

'Vicky, don't be rude,' reprimanded her father firmly. 'Just because you're a cuckoo in the musical nest doesn't give you the right to be critical of a love of music in others. Your mother would have deplored the pop stuff you listen to, but she would have tolerated it. As I do.' The pained expression on his face was mirrored by the rude face Vicky pulled behind his back, rolling her eyes to heaven.

'It's pop *music*,' she argued, 'not pop stuff.' She flung the present down carelessly and hoisted herself up on to the long wooden dresser where she sat swinging her legs and whistling aggressively.

Michael Cameron rubbed a weary hand over his eyes. Vicky was getting so cheeky, so much more difficult than Kate had ever been. Perhaps, after all, boarding school had not been the right choice. Yet what other option was there? He could never have afforded a housekeeper.

The kitchen door opened and Kate reappeared after seeing Adrian off. She was smiling to herself, a happy secret look that made Vicky feel particularly bitchy.

'Are you going to marry Adrian? He's obviously potty about you and you've such a big thing in common — organs!' Then, fearing she had gone too far, she rushed on, 'If he was teaching *me* in a comprehensive I'd mess about in his lessons.'

The vicar was really angry now. 'Help your sister with the rest of those dishes. And stop talking nonsense. Adrian may seem rather — er, quiet — to you, but I can assure you, young lady, that he's a first-rate teacher and would sort out the likes of you in no time.'

Vicky changed her tactics, trying to win back her father's approval. 'It would be nice for you though, wouldn't it, Daddy? If they got married there's plenty of room for them to come and live here. Kate could stop nursing and have babies and be at home all the time.'

'Really, Vicky!' Her face crimson, Kate threatened her sister with a wet dishcloth. 'For goodness' sake put a sock in it or I'll be sorely tempted to . . .'

A plate slipped through the younger girl's fingers with a splintering crash. 'Damn it to hell!' She said it loudly and deliberately, then before anyone could voice a word of reproof, flounced out of the kitchen.

Kate bit her lip at the look of perplexity in her father's faded blue eyes. It was so easy to see through

Vicky; why, she was transparent as glass. You could see the uncertainty behind the rebellious facade if you only looked beyond the dramatic words and actions.

'Don't worry about her,' she said gently. 'It's just the teenage blues. Vicky's trying things out, watching for our reactions. We've got to be understanding and tolerant.'

'I keep wondering,' her father spoke meditatively, staring ahead with fixed gaze, 'if our little Vicky isn't living out an emotional disturbance. A delayed reaction to your mother's death. She seemed to recover from the shock so quickly. Whereas you, poor girl, had to grow up overnight. You never had those carefree teenage years everyone ought to enjoy.'

Kate managed a smile. 'Adolescents seem to thrive on a bit of drama. If you ask me, they'd rather invent some aggro to relieve the boredom. That bit of swearing was definitely for effect.'

'Hmm, you may well be right. It's not easy to be objective about your own children — as one day you will find, my dear. He's a decent chap you know, Adrian. I'd like,' he ventured tentatively, 'to see you happily married, Kate. Though you're still very young — only twenty. You ought to see a bit of the world, meet more people. You mustn't put me and Vicky before anything you really want in life. Of course, it's a bonus having you home so often,' he peered anxiously at the averted face. 'Don't think I'm not deeply grateful. But I'd manage on my own if I had to.'

A pair of brilliantly dark eyes smiled into his own. 'Really, Dad!' Kate disguised her emotion with a show of mock annoyance. 'Is everyone trying to foist me on to poor Adrian? Why, I agree with you. I see my SRN as a passport to all sorts of things. 'I could go abroad, work on a cruise liner, take a nursing degree — anything. The world,' she laughed, 'is my oyster. But until I've sat my final exams I'm more than content to make myself useful here.

'And now,' she squeezed his hand in

loving complicity, 'let's find the tree decorations and give that monster something useful to occupy herself with. She shall have a Christmas to remember.'

So it was not until she climbed the stairs to bed that night, hugging a hot water bottle to her shivering body, that Kate found a moment for her own thoughts. The familiar shabby, comfortable bedroom was as usual so cold that her breath hung like smoke on the still air. Wasting no time, Kate prepared for the night, her routine finishing up as ever with fixing that thick plait of hair which hung down between her narrow shoulder-blades.

Then she hopped, teeth chattering, into bed, snuggling deep under the blankets, fluffy woollen bedsocks warding off those dreaded winter chilblains as the cold sheets made her gasp and remember the central heating of the nurses' home.

Sleep, though, was slow in coming. The white iron bedstead creaked complainingly as Kate tossed and turned in an effort to settle into a warm, snug spot.

Vivid pictures would keep storming relentlessly through her imagination, however tight she squeezed shut her eyes. It must be the cold, Kate tried to comfort herself, keeping her tired body in a state of restless tension. There seemed no ready escape from the scenes racing through her hyperactive mind.

Kate lay there in the dark, huddled against the cold into the smallest shape humanly possible, her arms clasped tight about her. Yet inside flowed a shameful warmth as the memory persisted, determined now to occupy the whole of her imagination, conjuring up so wickedly the feel of a hard masculine form pressed close, so close, to a slender compliant body.

Twenty-four hours ago I was like Cinderella transformed, she marvelled. Not a daughter, nor a sister — nor a nurse. And just look at me tonight in my grannie nightie and pink bedsocks.

What a fright you'd get, Prince Charming, if you could see me now! And you weren't really so charming, were you? Calling me a beanpole after making me truly aware of myself — oh, I have to admit it — as a beautiful, desirable woman . . .

Alone there in the darkness and safety of her childhood bedroom, Kate bit her lip. It all seemed so fanciful, as though she must have dreamed everything. And yet how could she have, when just by shutting her eyes she could all but feel that lazy, heavy-lidded gaze travelling over every inch of her; the unapologetic strength of the stranger's cool hands. Those hands . . . those eyes . . . and the fascination of that expert, dangerous mouth.

3

Kate raced up the stairs three at a time, long legs flying, drops of rain flicking off her shiny red mac. Inside her room she tore off her skirt and sweater and twenty seconds later was presentable enough for duty — apart from one vital item; her cap.

Struggling in front of the mirror she didn't hear the door open, and when Joanna appeared beaming at her side Kate gasped in surprise and almost swallowed whole the white hairpins clamped between her teeth.

'I've been *dying* to see you!' Jo's blue eyes glowed with excitement and her blonde curls bounced enthusiastically. 'What about that guy you made such a hit with, Kate! No, don't try and groan — you'll choke yourself and be down in Casualty even quicker than you expected.' She glanced at her watch, tucking it carelessly back into the pocket of her blue striped uniform. 'You're okay yet — it's only just ten to.'

Kate spilled the hairpins onto her dressing-table. 'You know what a tartar Sister Greenaway is. You've got to be early to satisfy her. And my hair's playing up this morning.'

'Old bat,' said Joanna fondly. 'But her bark's worse than her bite. Anyway, *you* should worry! I don't suppose you've ever been late on duty. I enjoyed my stint down there with her — you know how I thrive on a bit of drama. With Casualty at least you never quite know what you're in for.'

Kate, who was frequently subjected to a barrage of gory questioning from the bloodthirsty young Vicky, rolled her eyes in heaven-help-us fashion. Getting that dainty frilled cap settled securely, perched on top of freshly washed hair, was always a trial. Perhaps she really should sacrifice the lot, all forty-eight inches of it, after all.

'What I really came to tell you,'

Joanna helpfully reached down a navy cape from its hook behind the door, 'is that I've found us a flat and I want you to move in with me as soon as possible.'

Kate wheeled away from the mirror. 'But Joanna, I never agreed to! How on earth could I afford it?' Her jaw dropped in consternation and Jo giggled unheedingly, pushing her friend towards the door.

'You look like the village idiot, mouth agape. Now get along with you, Katie, and we'll talk about it later.'

There was no time for argument. 'Okay, okay. I might see you in the dining-room, but don't count on it.'

The two nurses hurried off on their separate ways, Joanna to C5 Women's Surgical, Kate to the Accident and Emergency Department of the busy Stambridge Royal. Once inside the spanking new building her spirits lifted and the old adrenalin soared once again.

How good to be back, to start the New Year in the job that she loved

— even if Casualty Sister had her guts for garters the first morning on duty. Kate grimaced, hoping it was not going to become a habit of hers, judging by the number of new experiences she seemed to be going in for lately. Ever since the night of that wretched ball and the 'new image' Kate Cameron.

If I ever hope to be a Sister myself — and I do! — I must watch my step and not start blotting my copy-book now, especially with Final Assessment coming up soon. Getting promoted to staff nurse will be the next rung of the ladder . . . if I'm lucky enough to be invited to stay on here, Kate speculated.

As she sped across the gleaming expanse of cream non-slip tiles she marvelled afresh at the change in hospital design. Why, Casualty nowadays looked more like a luxury hotel than anything else, as far as Kate, who had never set foot in such a place, could tell.

At this hour all was quiet and tidy. The night staff had made certain of that. Ranks of empty blue chairs waited for their occupants, who only too shortly would be crowding in as bread knives sliced into careless hands and the rush hour traffic took its toll of impatient drivers.

Heading across the building, Kate passed the treatment area on her right, lying beyond wide sliding doors that allowed the direct admission of stretchers and trolleys. A boldly printed notice instructed patients to press the buzzer on arrival and remain there until a nurse appeared to take preliminary details. Patients able to wait for their treatment were then directed to the reception area proper where, at a huge wooden carousel desk packed with records of patients' notes and folders, three cheerful clerks waited to process further information gleaned from their 'customers'.

Kate strode now towards a wide corridor which housed various consulting rooms and offices. Casualty Sister was waiting in hers, gimlet eyes on the clock, bi-focals poised at the end of her beaky nose, impatient to organise her team of nurses and get cracking on the interminable administrative work which went inevitably with her job.

'At last, Nurse Cameron!' She stared meaningfully at Kate, her look more effective than words. Kate hung up her cloak and joined the rest of the group.

'Sorry, Sister.' And black mark, Kate! she added to herself, meekly accepting the rebuke as her due. That starchy image of the older woman was, nurses realised well enough, a front for vulnerability. Here was a woman, an ordinary person, doing a very important job which involved actual lives. That her efficiency must at times be edged with starch was a basic part of good management.

Had Kate had any inkling how that day was to turn out, she might as well have countered the reprimand with a laconic, 'So what?' and got herself dismissed right at the start.

But cheeky Kate could never be; and

a fortune-teller she was not.

Within three minutes she had been despatched with a more junior nurse under her wing. It was policy for the older nurses to help teach the younger, and Kate was particularly valued for her gentle, helpful manner. Noticing the frown of anxiety that creased the girl's smooth forehead, Kate sought to reassure her.

'I remember the first time I came down here I was really terrified. I bet you haven't had a wink of sleep.'

The pale face under its heavy fringe of sandy hair uncreased like magic. Someone else understood after all! 'That Sister — she just terrifies me. And you all look so calm and in control.' Wide, admiring eyes fastened their blue gaze on Kate. 'Of course, Study Block's been a big help preparing me for this, but all of a sudden my mind's gone blank and I seem to have forgotten all the theory we learned.'

Kate laughed understandingly. 'Come on, Jill, we've time for a quick cuppa before the hordes descend. And while you drink it I'll try and convince you you're really going to enjoy working here.'

Neat and trim in her cotton stripe dress, one ear on the alert for sounds of an emergency, Kate filled in the daily routine which Jill would follow during her six weeks' module, reassuring the junior nurse that she would not suddenly be expected to take care of accident victims herself.

'Your main task, as Sister said, will be to familiarise yourself with all the equipment, make sure you know where things can be found and where to put everything away correctly. Keep supplies stocked properly and generally watch what's going on. Come with me now and we'll check the sterile trolleys before things start to get busy.'

Again the girl's brow wrinkled beneath its sandy fringe, and seeing it Kate grinned and patted her arm. 'Of course, this is going to seem strange when you've been used to the calm, orderly life of the wards. But you'll quickly get acclimatised and find it's sheer hard work after all and far less exciting than the ghouls like to make out.'

Later that morning, finding pause for a second or two of reflection, Kate tried to visualise the scene through Jill's eyes. That sense of panic had obviously eased, but all the same the junior nurse looked dazed and hypnotised by what must seem to her like chaos and confusion, speed, noise, smells, groans and cries. The department was crowded now with the ill and the injured, cluttered with their friends and relatives.

John Rudd, the Duty Officer, had been working all night and was aching to be off. With the nursing team and the part-time assistance of a young houseman, a junior doctor, he had dealt with a multitude of emergencies, ranging from two-year-old twins experimenting with pushing beads up each other's noses, to the hideous results of a smash on the nearby motorway. To

Kate's certain knowledge there had also been two deaths and a whole assortment of complaints and ailments, mostly treated and sent home, the rest admitted to the hospital's own wards.

John Rudd was handing over now to Dr Barnes, a cold fish if ever there was one, in complete contrast with John's genial and unruffled manner.

'A *clever* cold fish,' pointed out Robert, one of the two male nurses on duty. 'His stitching's impeccable, even if he *is* arrogant.'

Kate shivered. 'Then thank heaven for keeping me safe! I'm scared of arrogant, contemptuous doctors.' Intercepting a head-to-toe appraisal which told her clearly that Robert considered her in no need of improvement at the hands of Hayden Barnes or anyone else, she blushed with sudden pleasure. I'm getting to thrive on male attention, she thought — this will never do.

Dr Barnes swished aside a curtain and disappeared into cubicle four. Kate bit her lip, wishing John Rudd were back again. 'H.B. doesn't treat patients as people. To him, they're just faceless problems to be dealt with . . . '

'Fast and efficiently,' finished Robert cynically. 'I bet if you'd been through a car windscreen — God forbid! — you'd be glad enough of Hayden Barnes and his invisible mending. Hey up, what have we got coming in now?'

A rapid glance in the direction of the emergency doors took in an ambulance crew wheeling through a trolley, on which lay the still small shape of a child, swathed in a bright red blanket. A young woman, still wearing the apron on which she had hastily wiped her floury hands, clung to the little arm protruding from under the blanket and stared blankly about her.

'I took the radio message on this one.' Kate scribbled a quick note on a pad and handed it to Robert. 'Cerebral injury. Could be superficial but the crew reported some deterioration during the ride. Can you get H.B. along as soon as I've cleaned up?'

Robert smirked flirtatiously. 'I do love it when you're bossy Kate — it really turns me on.' He exchanged his blunt Yorkshire accent for a simpering voice, whereupon Kate thumped him playfully on the shoulder and turned to meet the ambulancemen.

'Wait outside, mother, there's a good 'un,' suggested one of them as the woman, her face almost as ashen as her child's, attempted to follow them into the emergency room. 'Injury to the left side of the head, Nurse.' This quietly to Kate. 'Unconscious now, though he was drowsy and irritable when we picked him up off the building site. Pulse is slow and he's vomited once in the ambulance.' As he filled in the details Kate noted them down speedily, then felt with experienced fingers, quickly locating the carotid pulse in the frail neck, noting skin pallor and trying to ascertain the degree of shock. All this would be of help to the doctor when he came, saving valuable seconds in an emergency situation.

The boy whimpered and moaned a little, drearily, bringing his mother to the doorway, a trembling hand pressed to her mouth.

Reassuringly Kate extended her own towards the frightened woman. 'Would you like to help, Mrs Cash?' she suggested, seeking a practical way of alleviating the woman's distress. Far better for her to be doing something for her child than eating her heart out with worry. 'Let's get Kevin out of these dirty clothes so the doctor can get a good look at him. You just take your time and tell me what happened. You did say Kevin is eight next week?'

Together they pulled the sweater, thick with brick dust, over the lolling blond head with its grisly disfiguring wound, the hair darkened over the left side, sticky with clotted blood. As Kate listened she checked the grazes which ran the length of the left arm and flank, superficial scratches, no more, and watched the child's closed face, nodding her head with compassionate understanding as the

74

words spilled out.

'It's that building site over the way from us. They was playing assault courses on the scaffolding and he slipped, our Kev. I *knew* it was wrong to let him but the baby needed feeding and everything. They said he fell into all that rubble, rusty old pipes an' all.'

'How far did he fall, do you know?' Kate asked, her tone matter of fact and casual. She placed a small pillow under Kevin's head to help his breathing.

The mother looked eager, desperate to minimise the severity of the accident, make everything all right again. 'Not far,' she insisted, staring anxiously into the kind young face opposite. 'Not far, only about eight or nine feet.'

Kate passed her a plastic bag for the dirty clothes to be put into and drew on a small cream hospital gown. 'Just hold him over to one side for me — there you are, my pet, soon have you right as rain,' as the child sighed in his troubled dreams. She cleansed the grime from his face, registering with an inner frown that the pupils were unequal in size, indicative — along with the drowsiness and vomiting — of the presence of considerable cerebral oedema. This young brain had taken quite a jolt.

'Kevin will obviously need to be X-rayed. But first I'm going to clean him up so we can see exactly what the injury is and the doctor can put in some stitches. He's wonderful, Dr Barnes. That cut above the eye will hardly show in a few months' time.' It would help the mother to speak positively of the future whilst swabbing revealed the extent of the wound. And the damage really didn't look so bad after all.

'It's terrible,' shuddered Mrs Cash, wiping her eyes on the apron she still hadn't noticed she was wearing. 'So much blood!'

'Don't let that upset you. There are lots of blood vessels in the scalp and they do tend to bleed a lot.' Kate pulled the trolley nearer with her foot, reaching for a fresh piece of antiseptic-soaked gauze. She continued to swab gently, uncovering several minor cuts to the scalp, two that would require attention apart from the cut above the eye. The hair was a mess of course, but that would have to wait to be shampooed when the stitches were removed in a few days' time. But it didn't take too much imagination to appreciate how distressing it must be for Mrs Cash to have to see the dreadful discolouration of Kevin's white-blond head. And Kate herself was finding it difficult to put from her mind the memory of that other head injury, way back in her past. What was the distance of *that* fall? Certainly not eight or nine feet; not from the saddle of a bicycle on to the unyielding tarmac of that fateful road.

And so, when the little boy had been stitched, X-rayed and pronounced ready to be taken home by ambulance — there and then — Kate's heart gave a lurch of disbelief.

'You-you're not going to admit Kevin for overnight observation?' she queried, thinking she must have misheard Hayden Barnes. The direct stare of transparent astonishment caused the duty officer to pause and return that look with one of irritation.

'Why should I?' He peeled off his surgical gloves and tossed them neatly into the bin. 'The boy's conscious now and,' he nodded toward the X-ray viewing screen, 'there was no evidence of bony injury.' You had to take a chance sometimes, or risk having patients lining the corridors as the wards overflowed at the seams.

'But Dr Barnes, there *was* evidence of cerebral oedema. It's noted here in the records. That mother has other young children. She's in no state to check Kevin all through the night, every fifteen minutes for twenty-four hours.' Concern and indignation gave Kate the courage to stand up to the man she feared, but she held herself rigidly lest he sense the trembling that shook her inside.

The doctor glared back at her

through narrowed eyes. Give the girl due credit, there were not many who would wish to cross swords with him. And yet this one didn't look as though she'd say boo to a goose. How dare she challenge his decision!

'If I admitted everyone who is seen in Casualty, we'd have the hospital bursting at its seams, Nurse Cameron.' His tone was silky, venomously scornful, as though dealing with a fool who must be humoured. Steely eyes warned Kate to drop the matter there and then. Or else . . .

The child, sleeping peacefully now, dozed between them on the examining table. Gently the transparent eyelids flickered and — lest she disturb him — Kate moved recklessly to Barnes' side.

They had worked together before on many an occasion. He remembered her as a reliable and capable nurse; a good-looker who, rare among the species, used no artifice to attract his attention. The beautiful dark eyes were transparently honest in their direct gaze, but always veered shyly away if they should intercept any but the most professional of contacts. And yet, he recalled with a start, look who she'd succeeded in capturing at the Christmas Ball!

Kate drew back before the sudden gleam of curiosity which surged in those disconcerting speculative eyes. Her heart still hammered at her own temerity, her breathing was laboured, but she was determined he should hear her out.

'Dr Barnes, *please* won't you reconsider?'

Still those careful cold eyes registered with interest the rise and fall of her slim shoulders, the trembling of that gentle mouth, aware of her now not only as an opponent but as a woman. Yet to be taken to task by a third-year nurse who looked little more than a schoolgirl was intolerable.

The words rapped out. 'Listen to me once and for all, Cameron.' The rudeness was calculated, deliberate, final. 'It is *my* job to make the diagnoses round here, yours to jump when I crack the whip.' He turned away to write briefly on the case notes, presenting the astounded Kate with the sight of his implacable back. 'I will see the mother in one moment.'

Kate whirled and left the room. I don't care if he's rude to me, she told herself breathlessly, smarting all the same at the man's insufferable arrogance. But I have to do this because Kevin's my patient too, and I have a right to state my views and be heard.

She found Mrs Cash sitting wearily, her head drooping, resigned, quiet hands folded over the apron in her lap, eyes downcast in her private thoughts. At Kate's approach the drawn face brightened and the nurse struggled to return her smile with a confidence she did not feel.

'Ah, there you are, Mrs Cash.' She laid a hand on the woman's thin shoulder. 'Kevin is doing fine now, but that was a nasty bump as you know. So even though he's been X-rayed and stitched up very carefully by Dr Barnes, I think he ought to be kept in for twenty-four hours of very close observation. The nurses on the children's ward would check his pulse and temperature and breathing every fifteen minutes to make sure Kevin's going to be a hundred per cent well. It wouldn't be fair to expect you to do all that at home now, would it?'

'Oh, Nurse, how could I? Surely they wouldn't send Kev home right away? I mean, I wasn't expecting it.' The poor woman was hopelessly tired and Kate's heart went out to her.

She spoke slowly and clearly. 'Please listen to me carefully. Dr Barnes is a very busy man and he may suggest to you that Kevin can be taken home in the ambulance right now. But if it was my child, Mrs Cash, I would refuse to take the responsibility for him after an accident in which he lost consciousness for quite a long time. I am advising you to do what you have every right to do.

Ask the doctor *please* to keep Kevin here for the night, just to be absolutely safe.'

Dazed with relief, emotionally and physically exhausted, the mother nodded. Yes, she understood that she was herself in no condition to cope with a concussed child, who in any case should be receiving specialist observation. And yes, she understood what the thin dark nurse was telling her; she would beg the doctor to take care of Kevin.

* * *

It came as no surprise to Kate, the immediate summons to present herself before the Director of Nursing Studies and the Senior Registrar. Nevertheless, along with her determination to stand by what she believed to be best for her patient went a cold sickness which lodged in the pit of her stomach and turned her limbs to jelly. In the cramped staff cloakroom Kate splashed her skin with icy water and tucked into her cap as many of the escaping tendrils as would behave in response to her trembling fingers. Jettisoning her disposable apron, she hurried from the department, thankful only that Sister Greenaway was at a meeting and knew nothing of what had occurred.

When she had delivered the summons, Staff Nurse Bell had been more irritated than curious, chafing at the loss of one of the more experienced members of her team.

'I don't suppose we'll get you back before you go off duty, Kate,' she grumbled. 'No doubt it's to do with your allocation.'

Kate nodded in silence. Dr Barnes had obviously wasted no time but delivered his complaint straight to the top, not bothering to air his grievances with a mere staff nurse. Something Kate gloomily supposed she should be grateful for, though now it seemed as though even the routine post-SRN promotion to staff nurse might be beyond her dreams and hopes for the future.

A sudden picture of Kevin and his distraught mother flooded her inward vision as she hurried along the corridors, heedless for once of the shy smiles of slow ambulatory patients, weaving her way, deep in thought, through the flow of hospital life as it progressed along the wide arteries of its own circulatory system.

Unconsciously her hands gripped together in resolution. What was the point of standing by what you believed as a nurse to be in the best interests of your patient, if you were too cowardly to face the consequences — to defend your ideals in the lion's den? Kate smiled grimly to herself as she reached the suite of offices which housed the senior nursing officers. She paused, swallowed hard, took a deep, calming breath and knocked.

In her nervousness it came out far too aggressively, that knock; but there was no repeating the action, just as there was no way of undoing what had occurred down there in the emergency room. The Duty Officer must have his pound of flesh, and Kate knew she must be seen to 'bleed' satisfactorily, unless someone took the side of a student nurse against the powerful surgeon. But since there had been no witnesses there could be no champion — and the Senior Registrar would inevitably side with his own kind.

'Come in!' a voice rapped out and, with clammy hand on the door knob, Student Nurse Cameron obeyed.

The shock of what awaited her almost drained the dregs of Kate's courage. For the well-permed, tweed-suited Director of Nursing Studies was not alone.

There, leaning a casual elbow on one of a battery of metal filing cabinets, and clad now not in evening dress but the white coat of a doctor, waited Kate's partner of the Christmas Ball.

He glanced up as she entered — and, so it seemed to Kate with that other load on her mind, glanced away again indifferently. For her part, the girl was now so strung up it seemed impossible to behave with any semblance of normality. What was this man doing here in Miss Westropp's office? He could not have been expecting to confront any particular nurse, judging by the cool detached second when their eyes made contact — and parted.

Desperately Kate steeled herself to concentrate on Miss Westropp who now looked up from the folder of papers she had been examining. Kate's own records, she guessed ruefully, besmirched now by complaint against her.

As Miss Westropp very briefly made the formal introduction of a very insignificant young nurse to a rather important member of the medical staff, the new Senior Registrar, Kate's polite acknowledgement carried not a trace of the stunned state of her senses. And Mr Harvey's brief nod offered no indication that the two were not entirely strangers one to the other.

It was obvious that Cinderella without her finery had triggered no response in that towering, white-coated figure. Mr Harvey turned his attention almost immediately back to the sheaf of papers he had been studying, completed his perusal and handed them back to Miss Westropp, who in turn tapped them together neatly and housed them in their green folder. She picked up the telephone which shrilled its urgent request at her side.

Since there had been no invitation to take a seat, Kate was quite literally on the carpet. Not daring to look at the man whose presence had added a new constriction to her throat, along with the nausea in her stomach, Kate folded her thin red hands and stared at the mottled brown floor-covering. Her downcast mien allowed the covert regard of Luke Harvey, who had in fact received a considerable shock himself. The nurse he was intended to castigate was the very same girl who had danced with him the other evening! Damn it all, she just didn't look the argumentative, self-opinionated type he had been expecting after Hayden Barnes' impassioned phone call. And in uniform she was such a lanky slip of a child, with her thin bare arms and fragile wrists and ankles. Why, in the striped dress with its small cinched waist she reminded him more of a bossy school prefect, now raising her head with chin tilted stubbornly high, dark eyes daring him to challenge her.

But how fetching the wispy frame of escaping wavy tendrils, the becoming flush which heightened the pallor of the fine skin. And hers was a delicate slenderness — not a stick-thin fragility.

Luke decided to let Mavis Westropp start the proceedings; after all, it was her responsibility to discipline her errant nurses, his to represent the interests of the medics.

Miss Westropp finished her abrupt conversation, sighed exaggeratedly so that Kate felt herself to be the most considerable nuisance, put the receiver back on its rest and stared fixedly at the pink blotter before her on the desk. With her forefinger she rubbed the space between her eyebrows, as though staving off a migraine, then looked at Kate.

There were always two sides to any disagreement. It was particularly unfortunate that so assiduous and capable a nurse as the quiet, reliable Kate Cameron should be involved in an altercation of this kind; a clergyman's daughter too, the senior nurse recalled. How pretty the girl was — could that be at the back of Hayden Barnes' complaint? Had his eye for the more attractive nurses suffered a humiliating rebuff — for which he now sought revenge?

Not having been at the Christmas Ball, for Miss Westropp had an elderly mother who took up all her free time, the Director of Nursing Studies had no idea that Student Nurse Cameron and the new man might already have met. Indeed, the hospital grape-vine had much to catch up on after the disruption of Christmas and New Year.

She ran a hand over her silvery perm and nodded, not unkindly, toward the tense young figure before her. 'Now, what is all this about, Nurse Cameron? Please tell me, as briefly as you can, exactly what happened.'

At the invitation Kate began hesitantly, very aware of the third person in the room. She described all that had occurred, including the observations of the ambulance crew, her conversation with Mrs Cash and all that had passed between herself and Dr Barnes.

At one point Luke Harvey interrupted her, his deep voice startlingly unfamiliar — unlike his personable self. 'After your difference of opinion with Dr Barnes did you in fact go straight to the parent and advise her to ask that her child should remain overnight in hospital?'

Ah, she knew now where Luke Harvey's sympathies lay; if indeed there could have been any room for doubt!

'I did.' Kate raised her firm, pointed chin, defying Luke Harvey with eyes that brimmed with sudden treacherous tears.

He stared briefly into her stormy face, then hurriedly averted his gaze. Kate pulled herself together, furious that she should parade such weakness for his inspection. How stupid to care whether or not he took her part.

She had been convinced it was in the child's best interests, she explained fervently. One could not be too careful in cases of head injury. In spite of the superficial nature of the injury — as proven by the X-rays, the ambulance crew had expressed particular concern over the deterioration shown during their speeding journey. Over the radio link they had warned the hospital of the change they were monitoring.

'I see.' Nothing in the neutral tone of Luke Harvey's voice indicated whether he was swayed by her explanation.

But Miss Westropp's eye was cool. 'It is not for you, Nurse Cameron, as well you know, to make clinical diagnoses yourself. Dr Barnes had every right to raise strong objections to your attitude.'

'But, Miss Westropp, you yourself taught us that nursing means *caring*,' burst out Kate in dismay, wringing her hands now in agitation that her motives should apparently be so misconstrued. 'And caring means giving a damn and being human and doing what you believe is right by your patient!'

'And you think that gives you the authority to question a doctor's decision, Nurse?' The set of the experienced grey head was watchful now, wary.

But the young nurse carried on, recklessly fluent. 'You also told us we should not be doormats! That at the end of the day, when we've slogged our guts out, we should be able to tell ourselves we've done a good job — not let somebody down. Kevin could go home and be ill in the middle of the night and it could be too late! That's what happened with my own mother. They knew she had hit her head on the kerb but the hospital thought it was all right — and they sent her home. She died in her sleep that night! Don't you see I *had* to make sure that couldn't happen to Kevin . . . '

Luke's voice cut across the desperation in Kate's impassioned speech. 'Thank you, Nurse Cameron. Miss Westropp and I have heard quite enough now to come to a decision.'

Kate turned to him in anguish. 'Some of you doctors think you're gods and we nurses are just robots, there to do your bidding and incapable of independent thought. Well, let me tell you, I have a conscience and I will continue to do what I believe to be right — even if it offends you and Miss Westropp and Dr Barnes!' Her voice echoed within her own ears, sounding silly and hysterical — and typically foolish female, Kate realised with a shaming shudder. Still, what of it? She might as well be hung for a sheep as a lamb.

And punishment there would undoubtedly be, for Miss Westropp wore a look of disbelief at witnessing such an exhibition of rudeness from one of her own nurses.

'Nevertheless, you are a professional and must accept discipline.' The director glanced across at Luke Harvey, who was rubbing his chin with a stunned air as if he had just made a grievous error of personal judgment. Kate guessed that if he really had recognised his 'beanpole' partner, he had just gone off her in a big way after the insults which hung so heavily in the air.

The nursing director looked carefully at the girl who stood before her, tense and defiant and, she sensed, on the verge of a storm of exhausted tears. She sighed deeply, knowing where her own sympathies lay but conscious that Dr Barnes must be well appeased. It did create such an unpleasant atmosphere to have tension between personnel. The nurse would have to be moved elsewhere.

Miss Westropp re-opened the green file and took out Nurse Cameron's personal study plan. There was not much time left before the Study Block for Finals.

'Go and wait in my secretary's office, please, Nurse,' she ordered, but her eyes met Kate's kindly. 'Mr Harvey and I will sort this out together.'

She swivelled her chair round to face Luke, making a helpless gesture of apology with her hands, palms outstretched. A heavy silence hung on the troubled air.

What a resolute little creature, thought Luke to himself. And what a splendid actress she must be — the essence of desirable sophistication one moment, Florence Nightingale the next. I am definitely going to keep a close eye on this young lady. But what to say to the expectant Director of Nursing Studies, the redoubtable Mavis Westropp?

'I think,' Luke raised a thoughtful head, 'that what Nurse Cameron has just demonstrated is that the bad old days of dignified subservience are gone.'

Miss Westropp expelled her breath in a gusty sigh of satisfaction. 'You have examined her records. This is a potential gold medallist we are dealing with, an excellent and sensitive nurse.'

'But perhaps emotionally susceptible in this case, Miss Westropp?'

'Indeed. Her own mother . . . ' Artfully the senior nurse allowed her words to trail meaningfully, to let Mr Harvey draw his own inference. She was a wise and experienced officer and unwilling to see a fine nurse pilloried by the likes of Hayden Barnes.

Luke nodded thoughtfully.

'And if I may say so,' continued Mavis Westropp delicately, in view of the unknown quantity Luke Harvey presented, 'it is not untypical for Dr Barnes, excellent doctor that he is, to regard the human element as ceasing to be part of his concern.' Her straight, fearless look belied the carefully chosen words, carrying its own silent warning. Luke regarded her with increasing respect.

'Miss Cameron does not appear over-strong,' he suggested casually. 'I see from the records that it was stipulated before she was made the definite offer of a place in the training school here, that she should try to increase her weight . . . One presumes her health has never given rise to concern?'

A mere lifting of the eyebrows betrayed Miss Westropp's irritation and surprise. 'Never. Kate Cameron is a strong, healthy young woman. We look after our nurses here at Stambridge, Mr Harvey.

'Now I'm only too sorry to have had to burden you with this on your first day in your new post, but will honour be satisfied if I effect a ward transfer immediately?'

Luke nodded his agreement and stretched his long limbs, one arm striking the central light fitting and causing it to sway drunkenly. Miss Westropp's eye followed the movement as he caught the plastic shade with an effortless hand and steadied it. No question about it, more than a few hearts would be set fluttering at the sight of the fine, commanding figure of Luke Harvey.

A good thing I'm past getting *my* heart broken, Mavis Westropp told herself with an ironic grimace. And a pity there aren't *more* sensible work-orientated nurses like Kate Cameron, whose hearts and minds are dedicated only to nursing . . .

She pressed a buzzer and ordered her secretary to send Nurse Cameron in.

4

'We have agreed, Nurse Cameron, that it would be better for all parties if you were to be transferred from the A and E Unit immediately.'

Kate swayed tensely, waiting to know her punishment. Not that it mattered much really. Father was right; as soon as she had her SRN it would be time to move on, to make a fresh life for herself away from Stambridge Royal, away from home even. But what damage, she asked herself, would this unhappy episode do to her final assessment?

Plainly reading her qualms, Miss Westropp relaxed her severity. 'We do not intend to let this unfortunate occurrence affect your assessment, Nurse.' Her eyes smiled though her mouth did not, and Kate felt her shoulders sag slightly in relief as some of the tension began to drain away.

Miss Westropp continued. 'This has been an isolated instance in an otherwise impeccable period of training, as I have assured Mr Harvey. However, he may wish to give you a specific warning for future reference. Mr Harvey?'

Luke rubbed his chin in an attempt to look as serious and reflective as the occasion warranted. Only that the girl should avoid Hayden Barnes like the plague, went through his mind.

'Wherever you decide to send Nurse — er, Cameron, I shall feel it my duty to keep a careful eye on her, lest she further demoralise any of my colleagues with her very strong convictions.' There was a glint of amusement in his bold regard as he examined Kate's now quivering, suspicious frame and recognised her blushing, furious response. Miss Westropp was deep in her charts of ward placements and had noticed nothing of this silent interchange.

How humiliating! agonised Kate helplessly. First he makes mockery of me defending my principles — as if it were some frivolous laughing matter. And as for this pretence of keeping a *professional* eye on my work! How can Miss Westropp let herself be taken in so? Now wherever I go I'll be spied on, mocked and despised by him. 'Beanpole!' he called me — and I can tell he remembers! Well, I shan't let him see I remember too . . .

Miss Westropp had reached her decision. 'You should be going on to a medical ward again, but that's impossible at present. We will use your balance period to make up ward deficiency on Geriatrics. As from tomorrow please go to F Block and report for night duty.'

She could not resist a triumphant nod at Luke Harvey; this would show him her nurses were not hot-house flowers unable to cope with the heavy demands of geriatric nights.

Luke answered this with raised eyebrows in a so-be-it gesture and Kate, intercepting the exchange, could only assume that her destiny had been plotted between them; not an outright punishment for all to witness, but the hard nightly grind to remind her over and over again of how she had transgressed.

'Thank you, Miss Westropp . . . and you Mr Harvey.' Outward cool dignity masking her sinking spirits, Kate left the office and rushed straight to the safety of her own familiar room.

When Joanna came off duty and saw her friend's red, swollen eyes and heard the sorry tale, she was all in favour of seeking out Hayden Barnes for a piece of her mind — and a punch on the nose to go with it.

'He's a right one for upsetting nurses, our Mavis knows that. But most of them just have a sniffle and don't answer back, so it never gets to her officially. And as for Prince Charming being the new Senior Registrar, well — things are getting interesting!'

'You can forget the Charming,' hiccuped Kate. 'It was his idea to get me away from the unit. You should have seen the look of satisfaction Mavis swapped with him. And just to twist the knife he stuck in some nasty jibe about keeping an eye on me in case I upset any more of the doctors!' She blew her nose on a square of soaking cotton and gulped down the hot milky coffee Joanna had made.

'Kate, Kate, you *have* let yourself get in a state about this, you poor darling! You're just not used to facing chauvinist pigs like Hayden Barnes; you've been so brave but it's left you all of a tremble.' Joanna bustled round, hanging up clothes and tidying Kate's bedroom while her friend gazed into nowhere with a melancholy air. 'For a change *you* need looking after,' Jo continued briskly. 'There. That looks more like it.'

She plumped down, ruffling up the green candlewick bed cover she had just tidied, and regarded Kate with a rare thoughtful air. 'You know me, I'm a doer not a thinker. But it seems to me you might have got Luke Harvey all wrong — being so wound up yourself. Now, Kate, you don't need me to remind you you're a first class nurse. Westropp knows that and she'll have shown Luke Harvey your records. So I really don't think either of them set out to punish you. Okay, so Geriatrics is no big deal, but you'll 'give of your best', as the saying goes, wherever you're sent, and you'll not complain. Seems to me the poor fella might have been trying to cheer you up, put a smile on your face — roses back in your cheeks!'

A feeble giggle broke from Kate. 'Roses! Jo, I was so embarrassed! The way he looked me up and down it put more than roses in my cheeks. Poppies more like! I wish I could stop myself from blushing, it's ridiculous at my age, but I couldn't help thinking of what happened at the Christmas Ball, and I'm pretty certain Mr Harvey was thinking along the same lines as me.'

'What did I tell you! I bet he fancies you something rotten.'

Kate shivered in alarm but Jo was not to be stopped. 'Keeping his professional eye on you is just an excuse to disguise what he's really after. Your body! Your innocent virtue!'

Kate clasped her hot cheeks with shocked hands. 'You must be joking! I don't believe it's like that at all. I never told you this bit Jo, but listen.' Feeling even more foolish, Kate recounted the 'beanpole' episode and they giggled together for a few moments. 'Good job I'm not vain,' she observed as Joanna held her sides with laughter. 'Nobody fancies beanpoles and certainly not arrogant pick-and-choose medics. Especially the sort who look as though they've stepped straight off a Hollywood film set, complete with Bahamas tan.'

Joanna stretched her arms lazily. 'Well, if you're really not interested you won't mind if *I* give Prince Charming the eye.' Casually she inspected her nails while a teasing glance studied the reaction to her remark.

'I wish you wouldn't keep calling him that, Jo. Luke Harvey just happened to be new here, and I got taken up by chance. You're welcome to him. He leaves me cold.'

'Leaves you poppy-red hot, you mean!'

'Beast!' Kate tilted the dregs of her coffee-cup over the tousled blonde head. 'Promise to say no more on the subject or I'll turn you a delicate shade of mocha.'

Joanna screamed and leapt for safety. 'We shall see,' she crowed. 'I told you, our Cinderella transformation would have repercussions. You've got yourself noticed once and for all — and now you've taken on Hayden Barnes and given *him* something to think about too. You're famous now, our Katie — wait till word gets around!'

Kate stopped short. Could be Joanna was right about that. Still, hidden away on nights in F Block . . .

'How about this flat you were telling me about,' she said thoughtfully. 'It might not be such a bad plan after all.'

There was a decent-sized bedroom each, a bright little sitting-room which the two students had painted white and crammed with books and plants, and easy chairs covered with remnants of brilliant fabrics. They were both reading French at the university and their course required them to spend the next four months at the University of Montpellier, deep in the South of France. By the time they came back, Kate and Jo would have finished State Registration exams and be making plans for their own lives; for the time being the flat was a bargain because it saved the students paying a retaining fee to hold on to the place while they were away. And the cramped little kitchenette and shared bathroom out on the landing did not worry the two nurses in the least, since most of their meals could be taken in the staff dining-room and baths and showers were readily available after work.

Downstairs in the Edwardian semi-detached house lived two post-graduates, a scientist and a historian, who were, they were told, rarely seen. Men, the students said, renting two separate flats. Occasionally there could be difficulties over the one bathroom.

Jo reassured the girls that would not put them off. She and Kate could move in right away, and as the road was something of a backwater in the daytime, leading nowhere in particular but threading a way through to other tranquil, respectable streets, it was quieter for Kate to sleep undisturbed than in the nurses' home. And Jo, of course, could invite back whoever she pleased, and at all hours, since she had the place to herself at night.

Nearer to the exams, she reminded Kate, they would have a haven for their private studies; and Roz had said she would appreciate the chance to join them whenever the spirit moved her, though it was too quiet for the redhead in the ordinary way; too far away from the bustle and conviviality of hospital life.

Kate found she settled in easily to the unchanging routine of caring for the elderly ill patients. Remembering her first-year experience of geriatric nursing, it was not hard to take up responsibility as a more senior nurse now on F6. Getting to sleep in the daytime was the hardest part, dog-tired though she might be and quiet though the flat was. A time for day-dreaming, for living alone with your thoughts was required before you drifted off into the sleep you had longed for that night.

It was an unnatural existence in many ways, but Jennings, the enrolled nurse, seemed to thrive on it. She was an enormous help to Kate and Cass Wynn-Evans, the second-year student, and somehow combined boundless good spirits with little or no sleep, since she had two young children and a husband and home to care for as well. 'Needs must where the devil drives,' she told Kate cheerfully. 'We need the money, Lord knows, and I *do* love my old ladies.'

Jennings, who appeared to have no other name, had worked on F6 for the past three years and knew where every last needle and broom was kept. Kate thanked heaven for Jennings. Cass Wynn-Evans was the product of a very superior public school; she made no effort to conceal her dislike of her present stint, complaining thoughtlessly about the inevitable smell which hung in the air and the endless bed rounds which exhausted all three of them.

It was as well that Kate was kept far too busy to dwell further on the events which had led to her transfer. F6 was a big ward with thirty-two beds arranged in two arms of an L shape, joined at the centre by the open square of the day room. The far ends of the L held the long-stay patients, some of them senile, all of them incontinent, fifteen beds in all. There were ten rehabilitation beds for patients who would return after treatment to their own homes and families, four one-bedded rooms for the ill admissions and any patient requiring isolation and the remainder for straight-forward admission beds.

Four nurses on duty would have been the ideal; on occasions two night nurses must struggle on unaided. For an hour, while two went to supper, the senior must work alone, her bleeper the only contact with Night Sister. Thus it was on the second night of duty that Luke Harvey discovered Kate making a slow patrol of the darkened ward and side rooms, her torch pointed downwards so that its beam could not disturb a restless sleeper. He stood unobserved in the ward entrance for a minute, watching as she guided a tiny person with two straggling plaits of grey hair, shuffling on bare feet, one arm encased wrist to elbow in plaster of Paris, to the lavatory. Watched as she patiently escorted the frail figure in its undigni-fied open-back hospital gown into one of the side rooms. He could hear Kate's calm hushing of the querulous chatty voice as it launched heedlessly into a shrill anecdote. Next moment Kate hurried into the kitchen and sounds of a filling kettle reached Luke's ears. One old lady was obviously not going to settle without her midnight cup of tea. He waited until the graceful, willowy figure resumed her place beneath the shaded lamp, reached for a copy of the *Nursing Mirror* and settled down to read until the next interruption.

When a shadow broke across the circle of her reading light, Kate looked up with a ready smile, thinking Night Sister had arrived in her usual unfussed manner.

Mr Harvey it was who folded his long length on to the wooden chair opposite and picked up the Kardex file, which listed each patient and the reports of day and night staff throughout the whole of the stay in hospital. Before going off duty it would be Kate's responsibility to fill in the comments for that night.

'How are you getting on here?' Luke

enquired pleasantly, intrigued that the clear dark eyes had filled with dismay at the sight of him. *Persona non grata*, obviously; a pity, but why? Did Kate Cameron consider herself so tempting a piece that he might be driven to leap on her, there, with only a platoon of feeble old ladies to spring to her aid?

This was a medical ward, not generally the haunt of surgeons unless a surgical emergency arose and the physicians required their services.

'Night Sister asked me to let you know she'll be late doing her rounds — there's a death on F3. I got called in to see one of Professor Hall's patients, a radical resection we did this morning — God, it seems aeons away! — who collapsed with breathing problems.' Luke yawned hugely and shook himself awake. 'Sister was concerned about you coping alone. So, as I was on the next ward, I offered to do a quick round with you here before getting off to bed.'

With an effort Kate pulled her concentration back to a professional level. Her voice emerged cool and small and stiff.

'Thank you, Mr Harvey, but I have just this moment checked all the beds. The new admission in one of the single rooms was a mite restless, but she's settled down since she was given a cup of tea.'

Luke nodded, flipping through the clear plastic sheets of the Kardex. 'Ah yes, little Mrs Froggett. Here we are. A Colles' and a Bennett's fracture, successfully reduced last night under general anaesthesia.'

So the spy had come after all. Kate bit her lip. Just as he had warned her he would — and just when she had least been expecting him. For how could Mr Harvey know Mrs Froggett was such a particularly tiny little lady? Unless, her eyebrows drew together in a frown of conjecture, he'd been watching her as she worked, spying as she took the old lady to the bathroom.

Now what have I said? wondered Luke impatiently. I don't seem able to put a foot right with this touchy young thing. 'Tell me more about her,' he suggested with casual interest.

Kate tilted her head, recollecting. 'Lily fell over at home. The usual story — put out her arm to save herself and sustained two fractures. She has also strained her back and is confused and disorientated. Quite a character though,' Kate couldn't conceal a wry grin. 'She lives alone and is *very* independent. I can't persuade her to call me when she wants a bedpan. Consequently, although she's a confused lady, I dare not put up cot sides and risk her falling again, trying to clamber over them.'

Luke nodded. 'If you think she's not going to settle, give her fifty milligrams Largactil intra-muscular. But she seems quiet enough now. Have you elevated the arm? Got her to flex her fingers frequently? That will relieve the pain and swelling quite considerably.'

Kate bit back an easy retort; *of course* she'd seen to all that, was familiar with basic orthopaedics. 'I

116

don't think her arm is causing much discomfort now, thank you. And we have followed all the normal procedures for nursing fracture patients.'

Why, oh why, didn't that blessed bleeper drag Luke Harvey out of her life and away from F6 in particular? Kate ached for the office phone to ring and summon him far from her side.

But Luke settled himself more comfortably on the hard wooden chair, picking up the *Nursing Mirror* and perusing with interest the article Kate had been studying on trauma units.

Reluctantly, Kate watched him from beneath lowered eyelids, her ears alert for untoward sounds from the darkened beds. Now was the first time she had been able to observe him unawares, at close quarters, while his attention was momentarily diverted. Her scrutiny became braver, her eyes lingered on the large, shapely head with its hugging crop of unfashionably short brown-gold curls. He must have showered earlier; towelled his head dry and come out into the cold night air from wherever he was living, for damp curls clung to the nape of his smooth brown neck and the collar of his white coat appeared slightly damp. He wanted to be careful, taking such risks with the temperatures below freezing, and him obviously straight from hotter climes.

In profile, Kate decided with a tiny shiver, he looked a hard man, Mr Harvey. Solemn. Almost forbidding. Deep, sensual lines curved from nose to mouth, carving furrows that reflected a determined will — and appetites which Kate in her innocence preferred not to dwell upon. The mouth was in some way contradictory within itself; that strict upper lip compressing the lower which furled with an aggressive thrust. The eyes were deep in shadow.

A fascinating face, Kate must agree, but one she could not like. Too assured and confident, its owner; yet another of those frightening professional men whose company made her feel stupid and unimportant. And who were all, so it appeared, after the one thing that travestied love.

Now if he had not been a doctor, what then?

Luke pushed aside the journal and leaned back into the shadows, legs aggressively out-thrust, hands linked together behind his head.

'I particularly wanted to see you.'

A cold sensation trickled along Kate's spine. She strove to appear unconcerned. 'Yes, Mr Harvey?' So, he had chosen this quite inappropriate time to recall their first meeting. She cringed inwardly at what was to come, pinioned there in the lamplight before him, while her tormentor was veiled in shade.

'Y-es,' drawled Luke slowly, all unwitting that he was stretching out the agony for poor Kate.

She drew one deep, determined breath. There was something Mr Harvey should know about Cinderellas, and that was that they had existences brief as butterflies, with no conscious wish to repeat what had been a 'once upon a time' experience, delicious and daring though it might have been. And it was no good Joanna predicting repercussions because forewarned was forearmed and Kate would make certain there were none . . .

Luke spoke from out of the shadows, and at the sound of his voice Kate's resolution was all forgotten. 'It's about young Kevin Cash.'

Waves of relief washed over her, to be replaced as swiftly by deep concern. 'He is all right now, isn't he? I haven't had a minute to pop down to ask.'

'That's really why I called in. I thought you would like to know. But finding you all on your own on this big ward I felt I should stay and keep you company for a while.' He shot back his cuff and glanced at the heavy gold watch strapped about his sinewy tanned wrist. 'I guess your colleagues will be back in ten minutes and you'll be going down to second dinner.'

'Yes, yes,' agreed Kate with uncharacteristic impatience. 'But what about Kevin?'

'He'll be going home tomorrow.'

Kate was somewhat taken aback. 'You mean the child is still here, in Stambridge Royal? I thought it was just twenty-four hours' observation.'

'Indeed.' Luke leaned forward, coming out of the darkness so that his face was clearly illuminated once more. 'But observation was extended to three days so as to be absolutely certain there could be no slow haemorrhage. Can't be too careful in such cases.' He was solemn now, no trace in his manner of that earlier mockery which had so upset Kate. Was it possible she could, after all, have been mistaken? What was it Jo had suggested? That Mr Harvey might have been attempting to cheer her up, to bring the roses back to her stricken face . . .

An enormous gasp of relief broke from her parted lips and one eager hand stretched out to clasp his sleeve in an unconscious reflexive gesture.

'Kevin's going to be perfectly okay then?' Her face was bright with pleasure.

An answering broad grin chased the years from Luke's tough features. 'One hundred per cent,' he emphasised, 'apart from a few minor war wounds.' It delighted him that this earnest creature should be so much more concerned for the child than with saving her own neck in that battle with Hayden Barnes. It was plain that her thoughts had not yet even registered that possibility.

'Of course, that well and truly lets you off the hook,' he suggested teasingly, and was rewarded by the sight of a delicate blush staining the white skin of her face and throat.

'Well, I'm certainly glad to know that, Mr Harvey. But I should be sorry to think Dr Barnes still thinks badly of me.'

Luke rubbed his chin thoughtfully. 'I don't think you need to worry about that. We doctors make mistakes every day, busy people that we are. Fortunately they're generally too minor to matter. And no damage has been done in this instance — except to people's feelings.'

For a moment silence hung heavily between them. Then Kate said tentatively, 'And people's feelings are not important to your way of thinking?'

Luke's eyes narrowed. 'That sounds to me like a leading question, and I refuse to be drawn when we have so little time. Let us save that particular topic for an occasion when we can concentrate exclusively on each other.'

Kate held her breath. A few minutes earlier she had been determined she wanted nothing more to do with Luke Harvey. And here she was on tenterhooks for him to suggest a definite date! What was happening to put her feelings about him in such turmoil?

But Luke was standing up now, quietly stretching limbs that surged with a vital, almost tangible, power. 'Don't worry your pretty little head over Dr Barnes,' he said patronisingly. 'Hayden's a professional — and fast becoming an expert in his field. One storm in a teacup won't upset his equilibrium for long, I can assure you. I'll just step into the office and write up Lily Froggett's medication. You'll probably be needing it later on. Goodnight, Nurse Cameron.'

Well! Kate slumped back in her chair when she was quite sure Luke was out of sight. Was she imagining things again or had she just been very subtly put in her place for so presumptuously thinking that a mere student nurse could cause a doctor to lose his cool for long? Luke Harvey had a remarkable facility for leaving with a sting in his tail. And for setting her emotions in torment!

She was lost in thought as she walked slowly through the grounds towards the heavy smells that drifted from the dining-room. It was going to take a while before her digestion got used to the idea of roast meat and veg followed by sponge and custard in the middle of the night. But you were glad of something in your stomach when faced with the heavy bed-round which began with dawn and could swallow up a couple of hours or more. The old days were gone when patients were expected to be dressed, if ambulatory, and breakfasted before the day staff arrived. It was enough of a rush just to have them clean and tidy by eight.

'Ill met by moonlight, proud Titania!'

Suddenly a figure materialised at her side and with a start Kate recognised her companion. She drew her cloak comfortingly about her, too startled to think of an intelligent response to such a cryptic Shakespearean quotation. What could Hayden Barnes be up to, prowling about in the early hours in his smart dark overcoat with its collar turned up against the weather, hands thrust deep into his pockets as he matched his steps to hers and spouted embarrassing lines at her?

'Good evening, Dr Barnes,' she managed tentatively.

'Good *morning*, Nurse Cameron,' he drawled back in that arrogant Oxford voice which had been so hostile when last she heard it. 'It is morning, in case you hadn't noticed.'

Kate found her tongue. 'And there is no moon — in case *you* haven't noticed.' Then, hurriedly, in case she had offended with her unguarded repartee, 'Dr Barnes, I am far from proud of what happened last week in the unit. At least,' she struggled to be completely honest, 'I have to say I would do the same again; but I do regret causing you . . . er, annoyance.'

They stopped now and faced each other, Barnes not much taller than she was but stocky, broad and thickly muscled, padded out by his expensive winter coat to what reminded Kate of Henry the Eighth's proportions. Another domineering man, she recalled with a nervous hysterical giggle which as quickly she turned into a cough, who was fond of laying female necks on the block!

A clump of dusty city laurel shielded them from view of the main buildings and there was no one else in sight.

'My dear girl, don't you know I thrive on contention?' smirked Barnes. 'But I also recognise that I tend to see a patient as a technical problem to be solved as fast as possible. It's a common fault with doctors, as we all know. Busy people having to make instant decisions . . . '

'Nevertheless,' insisted Kate unhappily, 'I hope you can forgive my rudeness in challenging your decision. I really can't bear to be thought badly of.'

An arm whipped suddenly about her shoulders, pulling Kate firmly against Hayden's bulk. Through the heavy woollen cloth she could feel his fingers biting into the flesh of her upper arm. His breath seared her ear and Kate realised at once he had been drinking through the evening hours.

'My dear child, you're much too sensitive. You must cultivate a second skin if you intend to tangle with the likes of me!'

Too true, thought Kate in a panic, wondering why she had ever wanted to be a nurse in the first place. But it was Luke Harvey who had the power to disturb her; and far more dangerously than the immediate presence of a threatening, vengeful Hayden Barnes. For vengeful Kate sensed that he was, in spite of that smooth, disarming little speech. He wanted something from her, something more satisfying than a verbal submission could ever be.

She tilted her head away from the direction of his hot breath, sensing that the doctor was dangerously drunk but not wishing to vex him all the same. 'Still . . . I'm very glad to have seen you and to have had the chance to make my apology in person.'

As she uttered the words it came to her in a flash that Barnes had in fact been lying in wait for her; and that it would not have been impossible for Luke Harvey to have tipped him off that she would be passing that way. And at that particular time!

Kate twisted out of the man's unwelcome embrace. What if the two of them were in league to set her up for some punishment, some sport of their own devising? Her breath came in short panic-stricken gasps and she shrank into her cloak to hide her agitation.

'We must have a drink together when you're off, just to clear the air — now you can't refuse me that. Friday then, here at eight.' Before she could concoct a reasonable excuse for refusal, Barnes had patted Kate in a strangely affable manner and was disappearing rapidly in the direction of the car park, well pleased with himself and the world.

5

By the time Kate had given the night report and handed over responsibility to the day staff it was long past eight and her stomach was yearning for coffee and a bite to eat. The locker room was empty, every nurse either on duty or already heading wearily homeward or to her bed in the nurses' home. Anyone wanting to use public transport was required to change out of uniform for reasons of hygiene, but Kate enjoyed the ten-minute walk and the chance to blow away the cobwebs of night.

At the end of her on-duty stint it was into the linen basket with her dress and the creased rectangle of starched linen which had been folded into a neat cap. With fingers that fumbled with tiredness, Kate zipped up her black cord trousers and fastened the buttons of her warm plaid shirt, stowing an anatomy and physiology textbook into the depths of her locker along with the white wool and crochet hook which Jennings was teaching her to master. One thing you *could* say for working nights; it did allow opportunity for study in the quieter moments.

The knife-sharp January air always helped to clear her head, but today Kate found herself in battle with an icy wind that snatched cruelly at her breath and hair, whipping loosened strands into mouth and eyes. Head down, she plunged into its buffeting, struggling across the hospital forecourt and out into the busy streets.

'When this drops we'll be in for snow,' grimaced Nobby Clarke as he manoeuvred his van-load of sterile supplies through the gates, waving at the pretty dark girl waiting to cross the road. Recognising her as one of the nurses he wound down his window. 'Wish I could offer you a lift, darling!' he called with cheeky commiseration.

'You look all in.'

'Hello, Nobby,' gasped Kate. 'I wish you could too!' She glanced up at the ominous skies and her thoughts reflected Nobby's prediction.

It saved bus fares to trudge the pavements back to the flat, and the blustery weather was welcome as it blew away the lingering smell of the ward which tended to cling to skin and clothes and hair. Kate inhaled deeply, grateful to fill her lungs with a change of air, even though it made her gasp and stagger with its arctic chill. She tried to walk steadily, but it was an effort not to reel drunkenly with tiredness. An elderly woman glanced curiously Kate's way, her face pursed with disapproval as though imagining the tall pale girl had spent the night doing unspeakable things. If only you knew, grinned Kate, weaving across the road. If only you knew!

Joanna was still in her dressing-gown, shuffling round the kitchenette and scarcely half-awake. She had, however, the presence of mind to get the kettle on and was soon scrambling eggs while Kate made the coffee and related her saga of events. 'So I'll have to stay on tonight, Jo. Hope that doesn't interfere with any of your entertainment plans.'

'Course not, you goose. *I'm* not the one who's pushing you out whenever you're off-duty. Lord knows, you pay your share of the rent! Besides, you're good company most of the time, when you're not worrying about other people.'

A look of pure astonishment settled over Kate's exhausted white face. 'Worrying about other people?'

Jo gulped a swig of hot coffee. 'That's right. Your father, Vicky, Luke Harvey, Old Uncle Tom Cobley and all. And now you've added Hayden Barnes to your worry beads. You'll get ulcers before you know where you are!'

Kate's hand shook and scrambled egg spilled back on to the plate. Suddenly her eyes filled with tears. 'I never thought of it like that, Jo. You make me sound such a bore. Here I am

— you're perfectly right — worrying because I've got to go out for a drink with this doctor! It's pathetic for a twenty-year-old!' She tore off a piece of kitchen roll and blew her nose punishingly on its ungentle surface.

Jo ran her hands through her uncombed tangle of curls. 'That's not what I meant at all. *Of course* you're uncertain of yourself where men are concerned. You hardly know any — in the romantic sense, that is. Give yourself time and you'll find you can flirt along with the best of us. No, what I meant was the way you put yourself last all the time; never ask yourself 'What do *I* want to do?' Always think of how others are feeling, considering their needs first.'

Kate bit her lip and her shoulders sagged. Really this was beyond her, she was too tired to appreciate what her friend was getting at. 'I just think,' she explained slowly, 'that you shouldn't do anything to hurt other people. That's all. So I . . . ' she broke off, shrugging helplessly.

'Have a cigarette. Yes, go on, you do smoke occasionally so don't try and tell me you won't have one now.' Joanna rattled the packet insistently and Kate stretched out a reluctant hand. 'Good job I'm not on till ten today. Now, about Hayden Barnes and Luke Harvey. You know I'm really rather jealous, never having roused a flicker of interest in our Hayden myself.'

Joanna drew deeply on her cigarette, eyes narrowed with interest. Kate leant on her elbows, chin cupped in hands, the cigarette burning idly between listless fingers, dreading, in spite of her determination to be firm with her emotions, the prospect of the evening to come.

'He's a very sophisticated guy, Dr Barnes. Rumour has it his father was something big in the City, rolling in money, in fact. It's unusual for Hayden to date a nurse; he usually goes for actresses and models, so you're privileged, Katie dear. But you'll have to watch him. He may be a cold fish in the way he goes about his profession but it'll be a hot kettle of fish you'll find yourself in if he really is interested in you *that* way,' she added meaningfully.

Stubbing out her cigarette, Kate pulled a rueful face.

'Thanks, friend, you're a real Job's comforter. But if I'm honest, I'm even more apprehensive about Luke Harvey than Hayden Barnes. I've stood up to *him* once and I can do it again . . . '

'That's probably why Barnes is so attracted. Not many of us would put our heads on the block like you did. We tend to do as we're told and not ask too many questions, so it's no wonder doctors forget we're there to work alongside with our own skills and expertise, not just to be assistants to them. Now if H. B.'s after a consultancy one day, he'll need to be wed first. The powers that be prefer married men, and I dare say a nurse is a better bet than an actress in the long run.'

'*Joanna!* I thought our Vicky had the

world's most vivid imagination, but if you're suggesting what I think you are, then it's high time you got off to the hospital and I cleared up in here and had my bath before turning in for the . . . ' Kate giggled. 'I was going to say 'night'' She jumped up with a sudden spurt of energy, born of desperation to get to bed. And when her head did finally hit the pillow Kate was fast asleep in seconds, a healthy physical relaxation which drained away all the emotions and tension of the past twenty-four hours.

When the alarm roused her at three, Kate flung back the sheets, shivering at the cold of the unheated room. For a moment or two she sat there on the side of the bed, collecting her thoughts, the heavy plait of hair falling Rapunzel-like over her left shoulder. Then she padded across the chilly lino to light the gas fire, listing in her head all the jobs to be done in the next couple of hours — shopping to be fetched, father to be rung, a letter to be written to Vicky, oh, and a birthday card for Adrian, twenty-four on Monday. Shampooing her hair had better wait till last.

The nearest phone box was on the route to the shops. The wind had almost subsided and a handful of early snowflakes danced cheerfully about her head. Feeling less cheerful than they, Kate dialled her father's number and waited for the disappointment she knew would be there in his voice — bravely disguised of course, but she knew him too well to be deceived. But as it turned out, Michael Cameron seemed determined Kate should not think of attempting the journey. 'You stay put, my dear child,' he insisted. 'The weather forecast isn't at all promising.'

'Can I hear someone with you, Dad? There's a voice in the background —'

'Ah, that would be Alice just passing me another cup of tea. She's been so kind, dear, tidying up so you shouldn't be faced with chaos when you arrived. And preparing my tea . . .'

'How good of her! Well, if you're quite sure about tomorrow. Though I'd like to get back for Adrian's birthday if the snow holds off. Can you tell him I'll probably come by train?'

The pips interrupted and Kate could just hear her father's voice before they were both cut off. 'Take care of yourself, darling. Goodbye and God bless.' The line clicked silent, and thoughtfully Kate set the receiver back on its cradle.

The afternoon post had brought a letter from Vicky so Kate made a hot drink and drew an armchair close to the gas fire.

School's boring, she read. *I want to leave and train as a fashion model. Everyone says I've got the perfect figure for it . . . Lucinda's off to finishing school in Switzerland next September. I can't be bothered with university . . . Want to earn some money . . . Buy nice clothes.*

And so on for three complaining pages.

Carefully Kate folded the letter and put it behind the clock on the mantelpiece. Then with a sigh she clasped her throbbing head in her hands, wondering what on earth to do about Vicky. Fervently she hoped it might simply be temporary boredom after the excitement of the Christmas holidays. And 'A' level work, she remembered with a grimace, was a routine hard grind to be slogged through — with the reward of those precious grades at the end of it all which could open so many gates to an ambitious youngster.

Not for the first time, Kate was overwhelmed with thankfulness that right from a tiny tot she'd had a goal in life; to be a nurse, just like her mother. Nothing, no, nothing, could compare with the satisfaction of doing a job you loved — in spite of the stresses and strains of the nursing life. Vicky, on the other hand, hadn't a clue what she wanted to be. Something glamorous and exciting, she would suggest vaguely when pushed for an answer; journalism or the BBC, perhaps.

Kate curled up in an armchair with her writing pad balanced on her knees, sucking the end of her pen as she searched for the words and phrases that might succeed in spurring her sister on. It wouldn't do to gloss over that catalogue of complaints as if they were too unimportant to merit consideration. She must show Vicky that yes, she understood and sympathised; but that part of growing up was learning to accept responsibility for your life, and that often involved you in doing things you really would much rather not.

Scribbling furiously in her haste to post the letter, Kate groaned aloud as the advice she was trying to couch in cheerful chatty tones came rather too close for comfort. The evening ahead with Hayden Barnes was something *she'd* far rather opt out of. But as Jo had put it, Kate must learn to be a big girl now!

* * *

With a sigh of satisfaction, Luke Harvey finally laid down his pen, flexed those broad shoulders and leaned heavily back in the swivel chair. It had been a long but absorbing day.

He stacked the buff folders in a pile on the desk ready to be delivered back to the wards. Each set of case notes now contained a concise account, handwritten in Luke's bold, black-inked script, of the operations performed that day in Theatre Five — plus details of the surgeons' findings and their recommended course of treatment for the wards to carry out.

And now — the glorious prospect of a night of sacrosanct, undisturbed sleep. The surgeon glanced at his watch. Time for a quick supper, one final round to check on the post-operative cases, then back to his rooms in Cavendish Gardens and that mausoleum to Lydia that the Prof now called home.

Luke sat on for a few moments, deep in reflection. It was good to be working with the Prof again, this time as the senior man on the team, unless Maurice Hall himself was operating. In the old days Maurice had been plain Mr Hall FRCS, Consultant Surgeon at the illustrious metropolitan teaching hospital where Luke himself had trained. Now he held the Chair of Surgery at the nearby university, with an academic responsibility for the training and examination of medical students, along with his surgical commitment at Stambridge Royal.

Lydia had not lived to see her father's rise to such eminence. Luke gazed into space, deep in the thrall of past memories — a blend of happiness and, it had to be faced, that searing tragedy which had robbed him of his young wife and driven him far away. Not to abandon his profession, but rather to pursue his vocation in the northern provinces of Kenya. Ruthlessly devoting himself to work in a manner which left not a moment's room for reflection on the past. Not a man but a machine; the taunt Harry had used to wound him — and with such devastating consequences.

Five long years.

And if the Prof's technique had lost none of its compassionate brilliance as together they had completed the day's theatre list, Luke had been secretly and boyishly elated to recognise that for his own part he was as deft and sure as ever — Maurice Hall's protégé to the core.

If the older surgeon would have liked to reproach Luke for abandoning the undoubted honours which would have come his way, he was wise enough not to give in to the temptation, simply expressing his happiness to have the man who was his son-in-law working with him once more.

Luke closed his eyes, not in pain now at the memory of Lydia but trying to imagine her as she had been before the ravages of disease destroyed her beauty. Tall, slender and magnolia-skinned, with huge dark eyes and that rich cloud of hair tossing about her shoulders. Laughing and vital and lovely, as in that one black and white photograph he had allowed himself to take out to Africa.

'Can I get you some more coffee, Mr Harvey?'

Luke's eyes snapped open, but his reflexes were as fiercely restrained as his emotions and he allowed himself not a trace of a start at this sudden interruption of his most private thoughts, glancing calmly in the speaker's direction. In the doorway a young nurse in theatre greens twinkled flirtatiously at him, her figure carefully arranged in a balletic pose. The surgeon shook his head but picked up a pile of folders. 'If you really want to make yourself useful, I'd be grateful if these could be sent up to the wards.'

The girl tossed her head but came forward, deliberately brushing Luke's fingers with her own as she took the folders from him. He turned away and collected his tie from where it had been tossed across the chair, moved to unhook his duffel coat from the peg behind the door, while the nurse, one of the night theatre team, stared at the strong bronzed throat and chest revealed by the half-buttoned shirt.

'You're quite *sure* that will be all?' she offered with pert emphasis — but might as well have been invisible for all the effect her offer had on him.

'Night,' he murmured absent-mindedly, strolling past the girl and out of the theatre block, preoccupied with thoughts of another.

Later, pausing to light a cigarette in the shelter of the main entrance, Luke's attention was caught by an incident which struck him as curious. For there, climbing into a sleek black Porsche, was Kate Cameron, the last person expected to be on amicable terms with its owner, Hayden Barnes.

Luke rubbed his chin reflectively. It had been Barnes who gave him the tip-off that his glamorous partner of the ball was something of an unknown quantity within the hospital's social whirl. A Cinderella figure who for some reason had chosen that Christmas night to show what she was really made of. Barnes had admitted, too, that he knew the girl from her work on the A and E Unit; that she was, 'Quite a competent little thing, actually,' though quiet and reserved from what he'd seen. Which made that transformation all the more intriguing.

Luke recalled with a frown that if Barnes had been at all interested in Kate as a woman, he had successfully concealed it in his conversation with Luke. Though of course, that had been but a short while before the unfortunate incident over Kevin Cash.

So, what was going on now? Those two were supposed to be at daggers drawn. Look at all the fuss there had been.

'I must be mistaken?' exclaimed Luke aloud — but there was no one close enough to hear. He peered into the darkness, cigarette clamped between set lips, hand cupped about his lighter flame. No, there was no mistaking the glimpse of her white, flower-like face through the windscreen, framed next to Barnes' swarthy, confident features as he swung the car round towards the hospital gates, the triumphant growl of its exhaust like that of a hungry predator, bearing away its prey into the night to be devoured at leisure in the lair.

With speculative eyes, Luke followed the departing rear lights until they had quite disappeared, then roughly ground his cigarette underfoot. He hoped Kate Cameron knew what she was doing, playing around with the cold-eyed plastic surgeon.

For Luke was convinced Kate must be fairly inexperienced in the ways of the world when it came to coping with determined and amorous escorts. Had he known just how inexperienced, he would have been quite incredulous — but he knew as little of Kate's background as she did of his. They were worlds apart in so many ways.

What Luke did know was that, in spite of his massive self-control, this little episode had had a ridiculous effect on his blood pressure. Fancy getting stewed up on behalf of some little idiot driving off into the night with a man who'd been involved with more glamorous women than . . .

Chiding himself for being a hypocrite, Luke headed for his own car. The Cameron girl was old enough to know what she was doing, and it wouldn't be the first time that mutual hostility had turned into something else . . . Meanwhile, he would save his disapproval for a more worthwhile cause.

* * *

An unexpected warm front had taken the gloomy weathermen by surprise. So, in spite of her father's qualms, Kate managed to get home in time for Adrian's birthday.

To her astonishment she had considerably enjoyed the evening with Dr

Barnes — once she'd allowed herself to relax and forget the likelihood of Hayden wanting to get his own back for their previous row on Casualty. All this masculine attention was enough to make any girl blossom with a new confidence.

Hayden had been skilful enough to play things very gently — just a fleeting butterfly kiss, a light brushing of her lips with his own; a promise of other dates and pleasures more satisfying, he hoped, to come. And he had actually managed to leave Kate looking forward to seeing him again rather than dreading any further pursuit of her affections.

For once Jo had been non-plussed. 'I expected him to be sporting a handbag-size black eye by now,' she admitted. 'Didn't want to put the frighteners on you, but I was a bit apprehensive. Still, if you're really intending to see him again, bully for you. Though myself, I think Luke Harvey's a much more exciting man.'

'If I thought Mr Harvey was pursuing me,' protested Kate, 'I'd run a mile in the opposite direction. No, all *he* wants is to trip me up in some kind of dereliction of duty, and get me into more hot water with the SNO.'

'That's daft. You're getting paranoid about the man.'

It did sound rather silly when you put it into words; the idea that a senior medic should stoop to spying on a nurse, just because she'd had the temerity to argue with one of his colleagues. 'Well,' insisted Kate defensively, 'how do you account for the way he turns up on my ward in the middle of the night?' She wielded the hot iron with a dash, thumping away vigorously at a linen tea towel.

Joanna lay sprawled on her back in front of the gas fire, taking all the heat, a glass of cheap sherry balanced on her generous chest. She shoved a cushion under her head and turned the fire to full blast, grinning thoughtfully.

'Mark my words, our Katie, you'll find out sooner or later. And I'm prepared to lay a fiver it's that willowy figure he's keeping an eye on, rather than your incredible dexterity with a bedpan!'

'Oh, Jo!' Kate's cheeks began to flame; it was far too hot in the small sitting-room with the gas right up and the iron heating away. She concentrated on the intricacies of a finely tucked ivory lawn blouse, smoothing the delicate fabric with sensitive fingers all of a tremble. Only two weeks into the new year and here she was, agonising over three different men. Very different men.

Even their kisses had been different. Kate found that curious and confusing from a biological point of view. After all, she thought, we're all made the same way. Why should one man's mouth stir her senses so much more than another? With pleasure, she recalled Hayden's gentle brushing of her mouth with his, setting her lips aquiver for more with that tantalising brief contact. Guiltily she remembered Adrian's enthusiastic, wholesome embrace, which had made her feel — well, hardly swept off her feet. Biting her lip, Kate remembered too that day of the picnic. How much she had wanted him to kiss her. And how disappointed she'd been when, in spite of her clumsy efforts to encourage him, Adrian hadn't dared to take such advantage of a vicar's daughter of brief acquaintance.

Yet when at last it had happened she'd felt nothing more than a warm and kindly sense of friendship. There had been no electric spark, not even briefly as with Hayden. Or devastatingly — as with Luke.

Breathing softly, her lips parted and dark eyes focused dreamily inward, Kate found herself longing — in spite of her protests — to see Luke again. The longing was almost as unbearable as the greatest pain she could think of; earache perhaps, or that time she'd trodden on a rusty nail and her foot had gone septic. A deep sigh escaped her lips. Would she see him that night, back on duty again? Was Jo right, could he seriously be romantically interested in a dark beanpole with enormous size seven feet?

Kate began to smile in anticipation, her lips soundlessly forming his name — Luke, Luke, Luke, butterfly tremors stealing through her as she imagined him taking her hand, leading her into the sluice . . .

'Kate! You're burning my blouse. Quick — lift the iron off!'

Joanna's outraged shriek brought the dreamer down to earth with a start. The shape of the iron stood out in singed brown across the fabric, and in puzzled horror Kate stared at her handiwork. For a moment she had quite forgotten where she was, what she was supposed to be doing! Then, after that split, frozen second of disbelief, she flew into action and within seconds had the garment steeping in a bowl of milk, pouring out profuse apologies the while and vowing to replace the blouse with an identical model.

'Oh yeah?' said Joanna in tones of mild exasperation. 'That was hand-made in France and would take a month of our salaries put together. You remember — it was a thank-you present from that man I met on holiday last year.' She gave her friend a long shrewd look. 'Penny for your thoughts. You were miles away.'

Kate bit her lip as she poked ineffectually at the soaking blouse, peering into the milky mess and avoiding Joanna's eye. 'Well,' she began lamely, searching for some glib excuse, 'I *was* dreaming a bit . . . '

' . . . About a man. Or *men*, I can guess. Well folks, it had to happen. All this time and Miss Kate Cameron has never felt the need for an emotional attachment. Now the offers are pouring in and she doesn't know who to go for. Look at my poor blouse — these men certainly have a lot to answer for!' Jo poured herself another glass of sherry in consolation and settled down again before the fire.

'Well,' said Kate with a show of spirit, 'you could try doing your own ironing for a change. I'm sick of playing Martha to your Mary.'

'Attagirl, I quite agree! Though it's a small price to pay in exchange for the pearls of my wisdom. Don't think I quite qualify for the role of Wise Virgin though; playing Mary to your Martha sounds much more appealing.'

Both girls dissolved into laughter and Kate caught herself smiling at the memory later, while her busy hands prepared the medicine trolley. She locked the drugs cupboard, checked it was secure, stowed the keys safely inside her uniform pocket and collected a jug of fresh water from the kitchen tap. Then, calling the junior to help her, Kate began the evening round of medicines and sleeping drugs.

They halted at the end of the first bed in which a woman in her early seventies, grossly obese in spite of her strict hospital diet, lay propped against a mound of supporting pillows. White hair cropped in a short, girlish style surrounded petulant wobbling red features.

Kate made a real effort to be nice. Mrs Lee was a difficult woman and it was more than likely she'd got a packet of chocolate biscuits stuffed down among the sheets. Her relatives would never learn.

'Would you like something to help you sleep, my dear?'

'What do you think?' snapped the woman grumpily. 'How do you expect me to get any rest when that one over there snores half the night? I'll have two of my tablets and a fresh glass of water. This one's got bubbles in it and that means it's stale.'

'Good evening, Nurses.' The cheerful voice of Kate's favourite among the night sisters rang out as Sister Mills strode into the F6 corridor. 'And where d'you think you're going, Mrs Froggett?'

A night-gowned figure was approaching slowly, shuffling along, one arm in plaster of Paris. A straggling grey pigtail hung down Lily's humpy old back. She wrinkled her beaky nose and beamed at Sister Mills. 'Hello, Sister. Aren't I doing well?'

Sister clicked her tongue with disapproval. 'Someone should be with you, Lily. And where's her dressing-gown, Nurse?'

Kate treated the old lady to a mock-reproachful shake of the head.

'Couldn't wait, me duck,' Lily cackled, winking naughtily back at Kate under Sister's amused but concerned eye. 'Thought I'd take meself and save someone else the bother. Nursie did ask me to wait a mo till she'd finished the medicines — don't want to see my little girl in trouble over me.' She beamed up at Kate, who towered way over her tiny frame, and reached out to grasp Sister Mills' navy sleeve in emphasis. Sister was just in time to grab her as Lily tottered precariously, while Kate slipped off to fetch the striped dressing-gown Lily should have put on first. Together they drew one sleeve over the good arm, tying the robe securely about the patient's middle. Sister moved on to make her round while Kate supervised Lily's 'visit'.

'Come on then, Lily, let's get you where you want to be.' Lily allowed herself to be ensconced on her throne, then waved Kate away with her undamaged arm. 'Leave me be now, Nursie. I can't perform before an audience.'

'*You?* You're always performing,' laughed Kate. 'All right, but you must stay there till I come back. And that's an order, young Lily.'

She disappeared to take a quick peep at Miss Jones, who was very ill and appeared to be sinking into a coma. Jennings was sitting with her in the dimly-lit side ward, stroking the still, frail hand, her crochet forgotten in her lap.

Kate gazed down on the narrow shape beneath the green hospital coverlet, her fingers feeling gently for the thready pulse. 'Soon as I get a moment I'll take over from you,' she whispered. 'Did Miss Jones take any of that warm milk?'

Jennings looked at the feeding cup and shook her head. 'She's not making any effort to swallow. But I'll keep trying.'

The junior popped a worried face round the door.

'Did you know there's a leaky pipe in that end cubicle next to the bathroom?'

Raising a finger to her lips, Kate came out to join her in the passage. 'Can you take Lily back to bed while I have a look?'

Sure enough, water was trickling down the wall from one of the pipes, just within Kate's reach if she stood on tiptoe. Tutting to herself over the rusting joints and flakes of crumbling green paint which showered down on to her cap, Kate felt gingerly along the pipes, trying to locate the leaking spot. To her dismay, what had been just a trickle now turned into a gushing flow, pouring tepid water right down her front and thoroughly soaking the nurse caught helplessly in its path.

'Damn and blast!' muttered Kate to herself. 'I daren't let go or there'll be an almighty flood . . . Nothing for it but to try and push the piping back into position. Jennings — *Jennings!*'

'Cripes!' echoed Jennings when she saw the plight Kate was in. 'Hold on while I ring the Night Porter — there must be an emergency plumber around.'

'Make it quick as you can,' gasped Kate. 'My arms are killing me.' The effort of keeping her arms raised high overhead was making her temples sing, but she pressed her forehead against the cold tiled wall and willed herself not to turn dizzy.

Then, miraculously, she felt the close contact of another body against hers as a third hand appeared between her own, grasping the pipe while a strong arm twined about her waist, lifting her clear of the downpour.

Kate slumped, panting, against a dry

surface. 'Luke!' she gasped. 'Oh, Luke — am I glad to see you!'

'Makes a change,' came the laconic reply as Mr Harvey did crafty things with crêpe bandages and a roller towel. 'There — that should stem the floods until someone more competent than me gets here.'

He stepped back to survey his handiwork, then turned an amused eye on Kate, noting her soaking clothing and the deliberate way she was avoiding meeting his gaze.

For Kate was uncomfortably aware that she had inadvertently and in the heat of the moment committed the most embarrassing *faux pas*. Quite openly and unmistakably she had used his Christian name. Her insides squirmed at what he must consider her temerity. Why, at the worst he must surely realise that in her private thoughts he was 'Luke' — just as though she could claim to know him, a senior colleague, personally as a friend.

He raised an eyebrow, inwardly

enjoying the sight of a rising blush stealing up from Kate's neck. He reached out and with a fastidious pincer-like gesture of thumb and fore-finger, plucked off the sodden cap — which had ended up over Kate's right ear. She snatched it from him, deeply conscious of the dishevelled appearance she must be presenting.

The young nurse's embarrassment afforded a chance to tease that Mr Harvey simply could not resist. He thrust his hands deep into his white coat pockets and masked the laughter inside him with a coolly deliberate once-over.

'How fortunate I *spied* your predicament, Nurse Cameron,' he said with meaningful grave formality. 'Mind you,' he went on, 'things would have been a darned sight worse but for the fact that you're such a beanpo ... such a well-grown young lady.'

His unusually attractive grin was met with a look that shot daggers. 'Thank you very much, *sir*!' snapped Kate. So he'd at last twigged she was on to his

163

spying game. 'Now, if you'll excuse me, I'm going to change my uniform before I catch a chill.' She made to push her way past, but Luke caught her bare arm with a grip that hurt.

'Not so fast,' he murmured. 'I'll walk down to the locker room with you.' He ran his eyes boldly over the contours of her body and, soaked to her underwear, Kate quivered with tension.

'I have to be quick,' she mumbled. 'We're having a busy night.'

'As always. Well, you can hold on one moment, I'm sure, while I just use the office phone.' He sauntered soft-soled down the ward, leaving Kate glaring at a particular point between his arrogant shoulder-blades into which she would dearly have enjoyed plunging a scalpel.

In the flesh, Luke Harvey managed to be the most exasperating of men. It was impossible to decide whether to be furious, fascinated — or both, at one and the same time!

Kate decided she'd had enough of the man for one night. She would make a

164

dash for it while he was in the ward office. Anything to escape the threat of more of that supercilious sarcasm, however brief the exchange.

Noiselessly she crept past the room where resonant echoes of a deep baritone voice could be heard out in the passage, and five minutes later she was freshly changed and heading back to F6. Just as she turned the corner of the well-lit but deserted corridors, Kate was in time to see the swing doors of her ward punched open and a tall figure head angrily in the opposite direction.

A pang of compunction squeezed her kindly heart as she noted for the first time a spreading patch of damp white coat clinging uncomfortably to the broad and arrogant back of her rescuer.

Kate bit her lip. Mr Harvey truly had reason to be furious with her now — the troublesome, *disobedient* Nurse Cameron.

6

It had snowed in the early hours, sufficient to cover the pavements with a thick crisp blanket, slow down the traffic and delay the milkman on his rounds. Joanna had already left the house and there was no sound from the downstairs flats. Kate had the place to herself to sleep undisturbed after the long eventful night.

Miss Jones had died as quietly and considerately as she had lived, soon after two a.m. when the rest breaks were over and there was ample time for the unhurried task of preparing the body before the strenuous morning bed-round began.

Kate was learning now to pace herself, to adjust once more to the topsy-turvy world of working nights. No longer did she feel so shattered, so bemused when she came off duty, but strolled back to her digs feeling well-satisfied with the hospital scene and her own part in that busy, purposeful world. Like many another before her, Kate was finding a special liking for geriatric nursing, a deep satisfaction in caring for her helpless old ladies on F6.

Now she stowed her red PVC mac in a cupboard and turned on the water for a steaming hot bath to relax tired muscles and prepare her for a deep, healthy sleep. Breakfast would have to wait until the milkman managed to get round.

The water never stayed hot for long in the bleak little shared bathroom. All the same, Kate managed a ten-minute daydreaming soak, hair piled inside the frilly blue bath cap Roz had given her for Christmas. Drying herself speedily, she pulled on a clean but ancient pair of thick cotton pyjamas, cast-offs of her father's which would do for cleaning rags when the winter was past. The elastic waist had long perished-but a huge safety pin restored comfort and decency — unaesthetic perhaps, but lovely and cosy in bed with the over-long trousers wrapped snug about her toes. For the time being Kate rolled the bottoms up round her ankles so she could walk about in safety, and put on her corduroy slippers — hearing as she did so the click of the letter-box as the post plopped through on to the door mat.

Pulling on a blue wool dressing-gown with neatly darned elbows, Kate tramped back downstairs to fetch the post. Nothing for Jo, one buff envelope for B. Ryder Esq. — and a thick white envelope addressed to herself. Curiously, Kate plonked herself down on the bottom stair and ripped open the expensive quality paper. Whoever could be writing to her in that unfamiliar flamboyant hand?

What a nuisance you're not on the phone, she read. *I really enjoyed our evening together. How about a repeat next Wednesday? Suggest the Arts*

Cinema followed by supper at Antonio's. Stick a note in my pigeon-hole if you approve. Yours, H. B.

'Mmmm, I *do* approve!' Pleased with herself for the genuine warmth Hayden's invitation aroused, Kate folded the letter with a sigh of content. How foolish she'd been about going out with him that first time, getting herself into such a state of nerves; all those fears of being tongue-tied or made a fool of!

She tucked the envelope into her pocket and decided to take a look outside for the milkman. She was dying for some coffee now and a bowl of hot milky muesli.

Kate opened the front door and peered out. Bother, here she was in carpet slippers and there were the pints of silver-top right out there by the gate. Thanks to the snow, the milkman was late and in a hurry; he hadn't bothered to leave the bottles by the door in their usual spot. Kate stepped gingerly into the fresh footprints on the path, trying not to get her slippers full of snow as the wind tugged her loose mane of hair into a tangled halo.

Then, just as she had tucked two pints into the crook of her arm and was reaching out for the third, it happened. Disaster struck. The mischievous wind slammed the front door with a crash at her back. Kate was locked out.

She struggled back up the path, unable to believe her own carelessness. *Surely* she hadn't forgotten to put the catch on? . . . But no, she'd been too taken up with the way her social skills were vastly improving to have a care for such mundane tasks as slipping the bolt . . . And now the door was shut fast against her.

Kate set the bottles down in the snow and tried the side gate. That, however, was hopeless, for the landlord kept it permanently locked to keep out intruders. Anyway, in winter no one bothered with access to the miserable patch of scrubby garden at the back of the house. Even if she could climb over the gate there was still no way into the building.

Trying desperately to quash the rising sensation of panic, Kate swallowed hard. Wildly she ran shaking fingers through the mass of dishevelled hair already tossed by the playful, teasing wind. Don't panic, she told herself agitatedly, don't panic. There must be some way out of this, so keep calm and think. Think of all the alternatives.

Inside her reality began to argue with common sense. Okay, clever dick, what do you suggest then, stuck out here in night-clothes? Shall I sit here on the doorstep and wait till Jo or one of the post-grads turns up? Or shall I take a stroll in dressing-gown and pyjamas down to the nearest phone box, reverse the charges and call up the ward sister on C4, asking her to send Joanna back here at the double? Or would you suggest I leap out in front of the next car and beg a lift to the police station? Knock on the neighbours' doors and ask for a bed for the day? Lord above, what an idiot I am!

Shivering now, as the wind bit through her clothes, Kate peered round at all the houses nearby. Empty windows stared unsympathetically back; no curious faces, no evidence of a soul at home. And the snowy road stretched empty in both directions.

Just then Kate noticed the brick. Half a brick to be precise, but still a useful lump and perfectly adequate for smashing a window. Kate picked it up and weighed it in her hand, considering the bay window of the downstairs flat. Would I mind, she asked herself hopefully, if some poor soul in dire emergency put a brick through *my* window? No, I would not. Or would I? Am I feeling rational enough to make a sensible decision? Or will coals of fire descend upon me if I smash my way back into a house where I'm merely a temporary tenant?

Deep in her deliberation, the approach of a vehicle went quite unnoticed as it slid to a slippery halt by the opposite kerb. Only the sudden slam of a car door breaking the silence made Kate pause, brick raised on high as she drew back her arm to strike.

'What on *earth* are you up to now?'

Kate wheeled around, relief flooding through her at the sound of a familiar voice — anyone's, it didn't matter whose, so long as they could . . . but Luke Harvey! Her jaw dropped in dismay and it took a real effort of self-control as she bit back an involuntary exclamation. That embarrassing episode was too fresh in her mind to allow Kate to make the same over-familiar mistake twice!

'Good morning, Mr Harvey.' Could any sane woman be glad to see such a man twice within twelve hours — and each time discovered at a disadvantage? Kate's disobedient heart turned a double somersault within her ribcage. 'As you can see,' she managed with breathless poise, 'I'm in a spot of bother here.'

She dropped the brick to one side, where it plummeted into the soft snow, leaving a dark hole to show where it lay.

'When aren't you, Nurse Cameron?' came the dryly sarcastic comment. 'You'll be glad to see *me* again, no doubt. Now what is it you're up to? Moonlighting — or should it be 'daylighting' — as a burglar while tending your patients at night?'

'Don't be silly,' said Kate crossly, brushing brick dust off her dressing-gown as she struggled to retrieve a little dignity out of such a humiliating situation. 'I'm obviously not standing about here just to scare the crows!' Hah, that was a good move — to take the initiative in referring to her jumble-sale appearance before the hatefully supercilious Mr Harvey could get one of his jibes in.

'I did wonder . . . ' Lazily his amused grey eyes worked their way upwards from Kate's soaking slippers, evidently relishing her furious glare. An inward searing rage against the man simmered

174

ominously, but Kate forced herself to remain outwardly cool; was he going to help her — or wasn't he?

'You have a rather eccentric style, my dear.' Luke had obviously enjoyed his humiliating perusal; the wicked gleam in his eye suggested a most unflattering amusement at Kate's expense and the simmer within her surged to boiling point. In a few seconds Luke Harvey would be on the receiving end of a most unladylike outburst from the gentle, calm Kate. It seemed he brought out in her all the worst and most uncharacteristic emotions — but *I'll be ashamed of myself later,* she vowed, searching for the words to express her inarticulate fury.

Meanwhile Luke went on. 'However, on your very pretty person even the proverbial sackcloth could not fail to look becoming.' He made a mock bow, wellington-booted feet planted deep in the snow, hands thrust deep into the pockets of his camel duffel coat, smiling down at the slim, swaying figure gazing

175

incredulously up at him out of startled dark brown eyes. Deep spots of rose sprang up in the girl's pale cold cheeks even as he watched.

The fight drained suddenly out of her, leaving Kate shaken, cold and desperately tired. 'If you could possibly help me find my flatmate, Joanna . . . ' she ventured.

Immediately Luke was transformed into his busy professional self. 'Haven't got time for that,' he interrupted brusquely with a quick glance at his watch. 'And you'll get hypothermia if we don't do something about getting you into the warm.'

'Thought you'd never notice!' Kate was struggling now to control her shivers as the frost-bite finished making a meal of her toes and began to chew at her unprotected ankles. She hugged her arms close to her chest and her teeth began to chatter audibly.

'Hell's teeth!' groaned Luke. He took one step towards her, and before Kate could offer any kind of protest she found herself seized in his arms and hoisted into the air. A horn toggle on his duffel pressed painfully against her ribs and Luke's rasping breath was in her hair; but ten seconds later Kate was safely across the road and inside his car, wondering in truth whether it was all a nightmare — and if she would wake up soon and find she had not *really* been abducted.

'Where are you taking me?' she demanded in breathless dismay.

'You can sleep in my bed,' came the terse reply as the engine roared into life and Luke steered through the trails of compressed snow. 'I'm lecturing at the medical school this morning and I've got clinics till five. So I warn you, lady, you're not my favourite person at the moment — especially after last night. Not,' he added with relish, 'that you've much chance of escaping me now!'

Kate's heart gave a lurch as she recalled how she'd so cleverly, so she'd thought, avoided him last night. But surely he must be joking. He couldn't really mean he intended to . . .

She stole a sideways glance, expecting to encounter one of those slow, teasing smiles — to reassure herself it was, after all, just another of the surgeon's jokes at her expense.

But all of Luke's concentration was on the road ahead; gloved hands gripped the steering-wheel as he negotiated the slippery roads; the set of his mouth was grimly compressed. Undoubtedly he really was very annoyed over her behaviour in avoiding him. And considering the state of the roads, wasn't he driving horribly fast? Involuntarily, Kate's fingers fastened upon the dashboard. Yet in fascination her eyes kept straying back to that confident, determined profile, those sinewy hands so sure and certain of all their skills.

And she was expected to sleep calmly and coolly in such a man's bed! Perhaps an apology would offer some kind of appeasement for all the inconvenience.

'I'm sorry I'm such a nuisance to

you. You must be sick of the sight of me.'

For an instant Luke took his eyes off the road and studied the untidy bowed head at his side. 'Why did you run off like that last night? Do I scare you or something?'

Do you scare me . . . or something! thought Kate in sudden panic. Am I transparent as crystal that you can read my mind, haunt my dreams? To think I first saw you as some sort of Prince Charming . . .

'You do when you take your eyes off the road,' she managed out loud, hoping vainly to divert the train of his thoughts. Her cold hands clutched at the neck of her dressing-gown, for it seemed the journey was over. Luke had turned into a narrow street, drawn up beside a high stone wall and was pulling hard on the handbrake.

'You'll have to get out on my side,' he ordered. 'We're going through the garden to the back of the house. I don't own the place and you're a very unexpected guest, so whatever happens, you are *not* to leave my room. Now I suppose I've got to carry you again.'

'Don't bother, I'll walk. My feet certainly couldn't be any wetter.' Kate pushed angrily past him and stepped right up to her knees in a drift of windblown snow.

'You little idiot,' Luke's voice was resigned. 'Well — if you want to be undignified we can play it cave-man style.'

Strong arms whirled Kate around and this time she found herself flung over Luke's shoulder in a fireman's lift, as lightly as though she were a pint-sized featherweight instead of the unwelcome beanpole she knew herself to be.

Kate resisted the temptation to beat with her fists upon the broad back over which she hung as Luke strode through a winter wonderland of glittering, mysterious shapes and pyramidal conifers shrouded in their crystalline perfection. Under any other circumstances the experience would have been highly charged with romance; now it brought hot tears of misery to Kate's weary, defenceless eyes. They fell in dark damp blotches on to the rough wool of his coat, trickling down her nose as she endured her unceremonious journey:

They came into a small courtyard dominated by Italianate urns filled with evergreen azaleas and a glossy-leaved camellia. With a surprising gentleness Luke set Kate down and unlocked a matt-painted black door, turning to usher her through just as Kate was surreptitiously wiping her eyes on her blue wool sleeve.

'Good job it's the housekeeper's day off,' he muttered to himself more than Kate. 'I suppose you have had breakfast?'

Kate nodded miserably, her stomach protesting at the nervous lie. Following Luke's example she left her footwear by the Aga stove to dry, wishing she dare trouble him to let her make a cup of instant coffee.

'Come with me.' As if he could not

trust her to do as he said, Luke grasped Kate's narrow shoulders and propelled her up several flights of stairs, for it seemed to be a tall, narrow, Jacobean house she was in, along corridors carpeted in soft dove grey and furnished with antiques and fine paintings — oils and gentle water-colours. Once, briefly catching sight of their reflection, in an ornate gilded mirror, Kate almost groaned aloud at the wild-haired, ashen-faced spectacle that stared back at her. Yet she could not have explained why, for once, it should matter to her that her appearance should please a particular man.

Relentlessly Luke propelled Kate on in what seemed a grim silence, their feet noiseless on the velvety carpet. Suddenly he pulled her to a halt, grasped a handsome brass door knob, threw the door wide and nodded wordlessly to her to enter ahead of him. When she hesitated on the threshold, an impatient hand thrust into the small of her back and Kate was forced into

Luke's bedroom.

However, she found herself not in the bedroom itself but in a dressing-room cum study. The solid walnut desk, with its untidy mass of boxes and papers, a white coat and stethoscope dangling casually over the companion chair, had obviously been put there specially for Luke's use. Books and medical journals were stacked in haphazard piles on the wheat-coloured carpet. A dinner jacket hung from the picture rail, partly obscuring the rich dark tones of an oil painting in a golden maple frame.

If the rest of the house spoke of money and assured but unwelcoming cultivated taste, this room was relaxed and lived-in. The feel of it reminded Kate with a pang of her father's study. He never would let anyone clean it properly. Her tension relaxed with the memory and a grin spread over her tired features.

Luke pulled a surprised face. 'Have my horns disappeared then?' He rubbed his rough short curls with a pretence of regret.

The grin turned into one huge yawn. Kate indicated the room with a sweep of her hand. 'This just reminded me of my father's study.'

'If I'd known you were coming . . . Tell me, what does your father do?'

Kate explained briefly, uncomfortably conscious of Luke's eyebrows raised in surprise, and the inevitable fact that he was drawing the usual conclusions about her background.

'A vicar's daughter, my word! Yes, I do see — and you like to get home to look after him as often as you can.'

'That's right.' Kate stared back at him, chin held high, challenging that speculative regard with her own direct gaze. 'And you're in a hurry, so I mustn't hold you up any longer,' she reminded Luke politely.

'Right, right.' Luke came out of his reverie. 'The bedroom's through there and the bathroom's two doors along. Sleep well, I'll see you later. And remember, whatever happens you must *not* let yourself be seen.'

Then, leaving her feeling about six inches high, Luke was gone.

Well, thought a bemused Kate, he's certainly concerned for somebody's reputation — but I'm not sure whether it's his or mine! She bit her lip, nervous fingers playing with the cord of her dressing-gown as she stood there surrounded by Luke's things, his personal belongings, in a strange place she knew not where. Hunger had gone, and in its place came a dizzy nausea. Her head drummed with fatigue and all of a sudden Kate felt sure she was going to throw up all over the soft golden carpet.

'I must find that bathroom!' she gasped aloud. 'Three doors along — or was it two?' Gingerly she moved along the deserted corridor, opened a door and peered inside.

The sumptuousness was almost blinding. Kate's breath caught in her throat. The most delicate shades of mint and cucumber, vases of pure white hot-house flowers, a great downy four-poster with billowing curtains of lace and drifts of silken voile; and photographs everywhere — of a girl who Kate, sickness all forgotten, stared at incredulously.

'It's me — Kate Cameron!' Lips parted in disbelief, eyes bursting from her head, Kate closed the door behind her and leaned against its reassuring solidity. But no — no. This vivacious face was, in spite of its startling resemblance, that of a beauty, with laughing careless eyes. In the dressing-table mirror Kate watched her reflection, held up a large velvet-framed photograph to compare with her own features. Mesmerised, she picked up a silver-backed bristle hairbrush and tamed her wild head.

Yes, now you could see a definite likeness. But that was all, just a likeness.

In spite of the central heating she shivered as though a ghost might have walked over her grave. There was an eerie quality of stillness about this room, just as though the air was rarely disturbed by its occupant. And closer inspection showed that not one of those likenesses appeared to have been taken recently; that lovely woman might have been frozen in time like some fairytale princess.

Kate's sensible, practical nature refused to allow herself to be frightened or to dwell in realms of fantasy. Time she got to bed, or work that night would be impossibly hard; people had been sacked for falling asleep on duty, and the fact that one hadn't managed to catch any sleep was not an acceptable excuse.

Kate turned to leave. Then her heart almost stopped. For there, beside the bed, was Luke. Luke, in grey morning dress, gazing proudly down at the slim figure close at his side; a girl in her wedding dress, laughing happily towards the camera, her adoring husband towering protectively over her.

In the safety of the bathroom Kate bolted the door and splashed her cheeks with stinging cold water. So he was, after all, a married man.

And why not? Mr Harvey must be in his mid-thirties, and so attractive a man could hardly have failed to . . .

Kate flushed the lavatory and washed her hands, oblivious now of her surroundings. Quickly she walked back to Luke's room. She sank into a chair, head in hands, baffled at the intensity of her distress at such a discovery, determined to sort out the welter of emotions which held her close to tears.

After long moments of self-scrutiny Kate made herself face up to the truth. She had hovered on the brink of falling in love . . . in love with a married man. Causing anguish to his wife, bewilderment to his children. And unbearable shame and disappointment to her own father. What could be more dreadful? But nothing had happened between them, nothing Kate felt she must be ashamed of, apart from . . .

She shook her head feverishly, refusing to acknowledge the memory of that passionate embrace with the stranger, the countless times she had relived every thrilling second. That indulgence, that *weakness*, must never again be allowed to consume her thoughts. Never.

A new horror suddenly seized Kate. She jumped to her feet in anguish. What if his wife discovered her here? Why had Luke said this was not his house? What dangerous game did he continue to play with her? All along she'd guessed there was some mystery about him, some secret in which she had unwittingly become involved. What if it was the doctor's plan to use her against his wife for reasons quite unfathomable to Kate's innocent, straightforward heart?

For the third time that day she wished desperately that there was some way of escape for her from Luke Harvey. But without proper clothing it was just another vain hope.

By now, Kate was feeling appallingly tired. The effort to stay awake was becoming just too much. She staggered into the bedroom and, as if to give the knife a further spiteful twist, the first thing her drooping eyes laid upon was another photo of Luke' wife, a black and white copy, carefully inserted into a soft leather travelling frame.

Kate could not help herself. She looked once again on the laughing vital face at the bedside of a man she could truly have loved, then curled up on Luke's duvet and cried herself to sleep.

* * *

Movements in the outer room woke Kate to an alert sense that something was wrong with her world. At first she lay rigid in the soft darkness penetrated by the streetlamp's glow. She'd forgotten to draw the curtains.

Why am I feeling so sad? What has happened? Why aren't I in my own bed? she wondered in a moment's agitation. Then Kate closed her eyes again in torment as recollection caught up with her; lay paralysed while her mind struggled to cope and remain calm.

The door pushed open and Mr Harvey stood silhouetted against the study lamplight. 'Hello there, it's just after six. I wanted you to sleep as late as possible.' He came into the room and picked her dressing-gown off the floor, holding it out as though he expected Kate to climb off the bed there and then and allow him to put it on her.

She pulled the duvet right up to her nose and stayed put.

'I'll be out in a second,' she mumbled into its plump, comfortable depths.

Luke pulled a face, tossing the garment on to the bed. 'I guess vicars' daughters don't approve of men seeing them déshabillé,' came the wry comment. He shrugged and left the room.

Kate was grateful for the flash of indignation which restored her fighting spirit.

Under her breath she made a promise to herself and to the unwitting surgeon. Remember that night we first met? You hardly spoke to me the whole evening. I don't know why. You're a real mystery man. But now I'm going to administer a taste of your own medicine, Mr Harvey. Let's see how you cope with an incurable case of tongue-tie, she decided.

I'm not going to challenge you with your marriage. That's for your own conscience. You'll never know what I've discovered. But you'll use me no longer for whatever devious plan you've had in mind, spying on me, checking on my work. You won't ever wish to see me again because I simply won't communicate with you. And with this resolution, Kate took a deep breath and walked out of the bedroom, her head held high.

Luke was sorting through papers on his desk, stuffing a selection into his black leather brief-case. He looked up but didn't smile at her. 'Do you want something to eat? I could tell the . . .'

Vigorously Kate shook her head. It was the first time she had seen him in casual dress. Husky Shetland sweater and faded, close-fitting jeans. Even to herself she couldn't deny it — Luke looked wonderful and her heart turned over at the sight of him in the kind of clothes which emphasised that superb physique, usually hidden by his loose white coat. Although her throat constricted with loss she moved resolutely to stand by the door.

'Hey,' demanded Luke good-naturedly, 'is this all the thanks I get for rescuing a damsel in distress? You want to rush off?'

Again Kate indicated with her head, eyes downcast.

'Kate,' Luke spread his arms in a gesture of bewilderment, 'what is all this?' Her name lay as easily and naturally on his lips as when she too had forgotten herself and unselfconsciously called him 'Luke' — and then been so ashamed of herself for hinting at a familiarity she had no right to assume.

The girl shivered then, remembering. But she'd not been wrong; her sensitive antennae had recognised what might exist between them, picked up those man-woman vibrations which Jo talked of so glibly. Kate knew she was nothing special; a gangling third-year student nurse, skinny and unsophisticated. But for some reason this heroic, clever man with his probing eyes recognised depths in her that had yet to be explored.

Nevertheless, Kate was resolute. She gave no answers but waited patiently by the door, hands clutching the lapels of the old blue gown, bare toes curling tensely into the carpet's velvety pile.

Luke was there in three strides.

He leaned over her, his hands spread against the wall, trapping Kate between them. 'What is all this?' he repeated in low, amused tones. 'Have I been sent to Coventry then?'

She turned her head to the left to avoid looking into those eyes which seemed to snake their way into the most private recesses of her being. Her cheek brushed against the wool of his sweater and it was all Kate could do to prevent her arms from reaching out and round him, clasping the solid warm body poised over hers.

'We-ell,' drawled the lazy, confident voice which tormented Kate's ears, 'if I kiss the vicar's daughter, she can't say no!' Slowly his mouth bent to hers, hovering inches away from Kate's trembling, hypnotised lips.

But a married man!

With swift grace she ducked under those captive arms, opened the door and stepped out into the corridor. Determined now, she was icy cool, a little fountain of bitter laughter welling up inside now that she had so neatly out-manoeuvred Mr Harvey.

She turned aside lest Luke should be aware of the softening of her lips, waiting with quiet dignity for him to escort her back to the flat.

Well done, Nurse Cameron, she told herself sadly. You've really grown up.

7

'Now you're quite sure this flatmate of yours — '

'Joanna!' prompted Kate,

'Er — yes, Joanna. You're quite sure she doesn't mind my staying the night?'

'Course not, silly!' laughed Kate. 'Why should she? After all, you've been noble enough to offer to sleep on the couch.'

Adrian indicated his intention to overtake the elderly car in front and moved out into the fast lane of the motorway. Neither of them spoke again until he was safely back in the middle lane, keeping strictly to a steady sixty an hour.

'You're sure you put those tickets in your handbag?'

'Gosh, you are a worrier,' teased Kate. 'Like the banns of marriage, that's the third time of asking.' She'd said this in a 'churchey' voice and was immediately aware of a sudden tension in Adrian that tightened his hands on the wheel. Oh lor', thought Kate, I hope he didn't think I was hinting at anything . . . How embarrassing, especially when staying single is all I'm determined to do — for the next few years anyway. Adrian is a darling, but there's no Prince Charming, alias Mr Right, in *my* life.

Determinedly she thrust away the mental picture of a tall, white-coated figure striding away from her down a corridor, a patch of spreading damp between the man's confident broad shoulders.

'You'll end up with ulcers by the time you're thirty,' she observed mildly. 'The tickets are right here, safe in my keeping.'

'All the same, Kate, I'd be awfully grateful if you'd just check. There's always the first time to make a mistake.'

Obediently Kate opened her handbag. 'Anything to put your mind at rest, dear Adrian. Yes, here we are. February 3rd at 7.30 p.m. Row F, seats eleven and twelve. City Hall, Beethoven night.' She wriggled with spontaneous pleasure. 'You know, this is a lovely idea of yours and I can't *tell* you how much I've been looking forward to it all.'

'We'll have supper somewhere nice afterwards,' he urged enthusiastically. 'I must say, Kate, it's great being with you like this. I want you to have a wonderful evening, one we shall both remember.'

The Mini in front was going just that bit too slow, even for a careful driver like Adrian. Once again it needed all his concentration for the task of getting past and back into lane. He barely noticed how Kate had gone strangely quiet.

Surreptitiously she opened her bag again and peeped inside. To think she had almost forgotten, after all that agonising.

But there it still was, that letter. Without opening it she could read off the terse contents from memory.

I shall be away at a conference for the next four days. You may rely upon it that I intend to see you immediately I return. L. H.

Short and to the point. Threatening words from a man used and determined to get his own way, a man who would not be thwarted.

Kate plucked with nervous fingers at her bottom lip, wondering how on earth she was to avoid the contact with him she had sworn never to allow herself. Luke Harvey was the most formidable of men. There was not the remotest chance he would change his mind — or forget. Her only hope was to evade him in the hospital maze with which she was so much more familiar. That way the surgeon would be less able to embroil her in argument.

Her deeply troubled sigh had not escaped Adrian. His eyes were glued to the road ahead but one hand left the wheel and squeezed hers. 'I'm not going too fast for you? You don't feel car-sick?'

Kate snapped fast the clasp of her bag and stowed it away. For Adrian's sake she forced brightness into her smile and warmth into her voice. 'Goodness, no! Just something I remembered I have to do that's a bit of a nuisance — nothing to worry us about though. No, I feel marvellous and I'm never travel sick. We'll grab a bite of tea at the flat; you can meet Jo and unpack your things, have a wash and brush-up before it's time to set off for the City Hall.'

A daring hand reached down and squeezed Kate's knee for the briefest of seconds. 'It *is* lovely to see you again, Kate. I've missed you not coming down so often . . . began to think you must have another boyfriend up there at the hospital.' Adrian cleared his throat with an embarrassed little cough.

'Who, me?' Even to her own ears Kate's voice was high with strain. 'Well, of course, I do go out with medics from time to time. Nothing serious though, just the odd dinner date or party.'

Adrian felt subdued. How was a

schoolteacher musician supposed to compete with men who held the power of life and death in their hands? And doctors were notoriously attractive to women . . .

'With the doctors, you say,' he repeated slowly.

'Well, yes, usually. But just on a light-hearted basis.' Kate cringed at the lie. True, she had never actually been on a date with Mr Harvey, but her feelings for him were about as innocent and light-hearted as Juliet's for her Romeo.

They were coming now to the outskirts of the city and it required all Adrian's concentration to sort out the maze of junctions and exits. Kate was grateful for the diversion of his attention away from her private-life to negotiating the more immediate dangers of the traffic.

Jo was waiting for them at the flat, putting on her usual 'Let's dazzle anything in trousers' show. Soon she was captivating a bemused Adrian with pert comments and vivacious looks, while Kate did her Martha act and raced around buttering scones and dolloping them with strawberry jam she'd made the previous summer.

'Gosh, real Cornish cream, you're spoiling me today, Kate!' Her visitor beamed happily, settling back into an easy chair by the fireside. 'I must say you two have made this place cosy.'

While Jo explained that of course the flat wasn't theirs really, Kate poured Earl Grey tea into thick pottery mugs and set a rich plum cake carved into generous slices at Adrian's elbow. He was gazing now at Joanna as though she were the most ravishing thing he'd seen in years.

'I say,' he whispered when Jo tripped off to her room to find some photographs of herself and Kate in their first year in training school, 'your friend is absolutely charming. What a personality!'

'She's always been great fun, has Jo,' said Kate with an amused but wry smile. Perhaps if Jo could so easily overwhelm the gentle Adrian, her charms would divert Luke Harvey as well. Better bring him round too one night . . . Jo loved them all, married or not. Hayden too, why not? For all his money and sophistication, and stimulating company though he undoubtedly was, Kate knew after several dates with him that even if he really was thinking of settling down, she could never truly fall in love with him. No, there was no likelihood of her swapping the nursing profession for any man; dedication to work came first in life and looking after her father a close second.

Kate went into the kitchenette to refill the kettle for Adrian's third mug of tea. Jo sidled in. 'Darling, he's absolutely sweet,' she hissed theatrically. 'You make the *perfect* couple.' Kate turned the tap on more forcefully, hoping the running water drowned Jo's words from other ears.

'Yes, well . . . ' she said, guilty that

she could not work up more enthusiasm for someone who was so absolutely nice.

'What a sense of humour!' exclaimed Adrian admiringly when Jo at last left for duty. 'She must be such fun to have around the place.'

'That's Jo all right,' agreed Kate, feeling about as interesting and amusing as ditch-water. If her feelings were hurt by Adrian's interest then it served her right for not being a more stimulating companion. She vowed to do better, to see that Adrian's short stay was memorable to him because of herself as well as Jo.

'Will you forgive me if I leave you alone for ten minutes? I have to change and do my hair. I'm afraid we don't have television here but there's plenty to read.' She grabbed an armful of assorted magazines and dumped them in Adrian's lap. As she bent over him he caught her by the hand and pressed a grateful kiss on her warm, flushed cheek.

'Thank you for a wonderful tea,' he said simply and the contentment in his eyes tugged at Kate's heartstrings. How easy it was to give pleasure to nice people; people like her father and Adrian. She smiled back at him, dark eyes crinkling with liking.

'I shan't be long.'

In the privacy of her room Kate stared critically at her reflection in the mirror. Tonight, she vowed, I shall make an effort to surprise you, Adrian, with how nice I can look now Jo has taught me what to do. You haven't seen me with my war-paint on, so here goes.'

She tried a few of Jo's flirtatious tricks, pursing her lips into a provocative shape, head tilted to one side as she gave one of those come-hither looks Jo did so well. Sucking in her cheeks, veiling her eyes with long sweeping lashes; then suddenly opening them wide in startled ingenuity.

Whatever would Adrian make of this? She looked more like someone with agonising toothache than a disciple of

Mata Hari . . . Coy flirtatiousness might suit Jo's cute blondeness; it made Kate feel about as seductive as a clown with a gumboil! As for Adrian, he'd probably run a mile if she should wander back into the sitting-room and vamp him in such an inept fashion.

Her shoulders sagged and Kate slumped there at the dressing-table. You're useless, Kate Cameron, she scolded her mirror-image with a rueful grin: about as seductive as . . . as . . . well, not in Jo's league, anyway. The digital clock silently marked away the seconds before, with an effort, she roused herself once more to action. Well, at least she was becoming more skilful with the war-paint — which ought to surprise Adrian not a little. For the concert she would wear her best — her only — cinnamon silk shirt, with the straight fine black wool skirt and her long boots; and hope and pray the City Hall heating was turned up full blast.

With automatic good manners Adrian

sprang to his feet at Kate's re-entry. 'I say!' he exclaimed. 'You do look perfectly splendid. I shall be a greatly envied fellow tonight.' His candid eyes beamed admiration at the picture she presented and Kate smiled back at him widely and gratefully, her morale considerably restored by his obvious appreciation.

It was going to be a popular concert, a sell-out, with a famous orchestra and a conductor of international renown. Adrian had managed to get seats well to the front of the stalls behind the podium, so Kate had a grandstand view when the vigorous motions of the conductor sent his white baton flying into the heart of the players. But unperturbed, Sir Harald directed the music by hand movements alone, right up to the end of the second movement when the slender white wand was discreetly returned to him. This earned him a hearty ovation from the ecstatic audience and Kate and Adrian joined in with wholehearted enthusiasm.

'Isn't he *marvellous*,' she breathed in Adrian's ear, her eyes sparkling with pleasure. During the next piece he held her hand and squeezed it in time to the music. This was not entirely comfortable but Kate bore with it as the interval was not far away.

Adrian led them in a race to the bar ahead of the rest of the crowd so they could take their drinks and find themselves a quiet corner together. There was something he wanted to say to Kate, but the moment needed to be as carefully orchestrated as the music. And he hadn't reckoned on his companion bumping into what seemed like half the hospital staff from Stambridge Royal.

'That was our Director of Nursing Studies,' hissed Kate. 'Miss Westropp. She's a dear off duty, but she can make you feel really small if you're in any kind of trouble in your work.'

'Good Lord, Kate. I can't imagine *you* ever getting into anyone's bad books!' exclaimed Adrian, startled into forgetting his anxiety to be alone with his companion.

Kate went faintly pink and hung her head over her glass of gin and tonic; it was no good trying to explain all that miserable business with Hayden Barnes, there simply wasn't time. And anyway, she preferred to forget it had ever happened in the first place.

But Adrian was already dragging her away from the Circle Bar, up flights of narrow stairs and along passages, leading the way to the Organ Stalls. Tonight he had made up his mind for certain. True, they didn't know each other all that well; but what he felt for Kate could wait no longer, and it had deeply reassured him to know that there was no other rival for her affections. The two of them shared so much in common, and Kate was a beautiful girl, totally unspoiled and so kind and genuine. Adrian's heart was brimming over with what he firmly believed was love.

Sure enough they found a deserted

spot at the back of the organ stalls; but another five of those precious interval minutes slipped away since neither could resist the temptation for a covert inspection of the great City Hall instrument, with its banks of manuals and countless stops. Adrian's fingers itched to make music — and he all but forgot his purpose in leading Kate into seclusion.

'You haven't finished your drink, Kate. Sit down here beside me.' He passed her glass and Kate dutifully sipped the clear liquid. All of a sudden Adrian's throat was dry. All those carefully rehearsed phrases had gone straight from his mind and he felt quite extraordinarily nervous. After all, it was a major step in a man's life and you couldn't plunge in feet first, not — he glanced at his wrist-watch — with three and a half minutes to go before the second part of the concert.

What *had* he planned to say as a preliminary? Ah yes. Adrian peered into the contents of his glass and began casually,

'You don't get home so much these days, Kate. That's why I wondered if you were . . . involved with someone at the hospital.'

Kate tucked a heavy strand of glossy, rich-dark hair behind her ear, shrugging her shoulders with a tense gesture. 'It hasn't been easy to travel what with all that ice and snow. In February you run the risk of getting snowed-up, and then how would I get back for duty? Besides, Dad doesn't like me to bother when the roads are bad.' An uncomfortable feeling of defending herself against accusation of neglecting her father began to take hold of Kate. But Adrian's next words soon dispelled that tension — only to replace it with a very different sensation, just as uncomfortable as the first.

All unwitting, Adrian plunged on.

'And I suppose now Alice Rayner looks after him so well, you really don't need to worry too much over getting home.' Deliberately he avoided Kate's face, but the intention was to reassure; to demonstrate how her father no longer needed his daughter about the place. Leaving her free to think of marriage . . .

Kate sat bolt upright. She chose her words carefully to conceal the shock of being faced with what her instincts had already acknowledged. If Adrian knew, then it must be the talk of the parish. And in her heart Kate was well aware how glad people would be for their vicar to have found another partner to share his life . . .

'I hardly know Alice,' she said slowly, 'but I understand she's been more than kind.'

'Oh, I should say so,' continued Adrian happily. 'She's always round at the vicarage, cooking, washing, cleaning. She thinks the world of your father and I must say she's got a heart of gold. Everyone wishes them well, both of them. The vicar hasn't looked so well and happy for ages. He's quite lost that drawn look — you must have noticed — and everyone's hoping . . . well, you know.' So you see Kate, he added silently, that leaves your conscience free for you to think of marrying me.

With an eager look on his boyish, fair-skinned face, Adrian turned now towards his silent companion. What he saw, though, stopped him dead in his tracks. He'd made the most terrible blunder! Walked right over her feelings with his size nines, trampled his own chances — for the moment — into the dust.

Kate sat there stunned, her mind awhirl. Why hadn't Dad said anything to prepare her and Vicky? Yet perhaps he had. Perhaps she had just been too engrossed with her own selfish little world to get the drift of what those gentle hints and allusions might be leading to.

'I'm awfully sorry, Kate. It seems I've dropped a bombshell on you. I'd no idea, believe me. The last thing I want to do is hurt you, you must know that.'

213

He reached out and gripped the cold fingers curled loosely in her lap, his heart now in his boots.

Still Kate said nothing, gazing into space with a blank, shocked expression on her white face.

'I thought it would be a comfort for you to know your father was well looked after. Leave you free to live your own life. It can't have been easy for you to get through your training and then spend all your off-duty hours cooking and cleaning.'

The cool fingers within his own flooded now with surprising warmth, just as though their owner had suddenly come back to life again. Adrian now found his own hand being gripped and Kate's gentle, smiling face turned towards him, her lovely eyes gazing into his. She sighed deeply as if some private personal ordeal was now past and she could think again clearly. For a brief moment she leaned her head against the shoulder of his grey tweed jacket.

'It was thinking of my mother,' she

said simply. 'It was a shock to realise how blind I've been. But if things do work out that way, no one, *no one* will be happier than me. You're absolutely right, Adrian. It will be an enormous relief to know Dad's really happy again — and *properly* looked after for the first time since Mother's death.'

Boldly Adrian put his arm about her shoulders, drawing her slender body close to his. His chin nestled in her soft hair. This was how he had known she would be, unselfish as always: her sensitivity was admirable too, but you could trust Kate not to let her emotions run away with her.

'Kate, I do admire you enormously, you know. In fact,' he hugged her close, his hand caressing the silky fabric of her sleeve, clasping the thin arm protectively, 'there's something I've been wanting to say to you, to ask you — '

But the interval bell split the air with its shrill insistence. Kate jumped to her feet, tugging Adrian's hand and leading the way back to their seats as enthusiastically as though the conversation had never taken place. But during the second half her delicate oval face wore a pensive, thoughtful air and Adrian cursed himself again for his clumsiness, guessing she must be thinking of her mother's place being taken by another. It was bound to hurt for a while; but common sense — and Kate had an abundance of that — would prevail.

As for him, he had well and truly missed his moment, bungled a golden opportunity when Kate had been in dreamy romantic mood, lulled by the spell of the music, receptive and compliant. Still, he would try again.

'Beethoven's 'Pastoral' Symphony — your favourite,' he murmured, his face close to hers as the concert reached its conclusion.

His reward was to see her face light up with gentle gratitude as she smiled into his eyes. 'You *are* kind to me, Adrian. I do appreciate it.' And it was her turn to squeeze his hand and to hold on to it throughout the lilting harmonies which rang through the building. Adrian might not be as rich and sophisticated as Hayden Barnes, as devastating as Luke Harvey; but kindness in a man was a most attractive quality and not lightly to be passed over.

*　*　*

For once Joanna was treating herself to an early night.

'I'd like a bath,' stated Kate, 'and I'm sure you would too. The only trouble is it's bitterly cold in there. You go first while I tidy up the sitting-room. And here,' she threw Adrian the old blue dressing-gown which he caught awkwardly, as if unsure that she really meant he should wear the thing, 'put that on afterwards. There's only me to see. Better to look silly than freeze. Then you can hop into bed while I have my bath.'

While Adrian was bathing, Kate

made up the sofa as best she could. It was only for one night, and though hardly the height of comfort at least it did spare him a long drive home, or the expense of a hotel.

'Now it's my turn,' she said cheerfully. 'Hope there's a drop more hot water in the tank.'

'Oh, I didn't use very much,' insisted Adrian, anxious not to be a nuisance. He was rather touched to be allowed to wear her dressing-gown; it hinted at an intimacy between them he hardly dared to imagine. What a good job the other girl was there to chaperon them. If she had not been — well, Adrian would not have answered for the consequences. He was not as a rule given to attempting the seduction of his girl-friends, but there'd never been anyone quite as important to him as Kate . . .

He picked up a dog-eared copy of *Private Eye* and began to flick through it, smiling against his better judgment at some of the cartoons and articles.

Suddenly a knock, sharp and peremptory, made him look up in alarm.

Who could be knocking at this hour? It was after eleven.

Adrian got up automatically and opened the door, frowning. He found himself confronted by a cold-eyed figure in evening dress, a white silk scarf slung casually about the man's throat. Both men eyed each other in astonishment and some discomfiture, each wondering what the other was doing there. Adrian had quite forgotten his own informal attire. What did this very imposing fellow want at such a late hour? What right had he to disturb two young nurses living alone? He must want Joanna.

'Where is Kate?'

'*Kate?*'

Grey eyes, cold as chips of ice, swept over Adrian who, to his credit, was not easily intimidated by other men. But it was clear the grey eyes narrowed now with fury as they registered exactly what it was Adrian was wearing.

He for his part was shattered. This man had the gall to visit Kate at most unseemly hours and was obviously pretty familiar with the most intimate articles of her wardrobe. Yet she had told him, had *assured* him —

'Would you mind telling her Mr Harvey called!' Luke rapped out the words with such bitterness that Adrian was appalled. What game was Kate playing at, stringing the two of them along in this way? With heaven knew how many others on the hook besides . . .

Luke Harvey turned on his heel and was about to retrace his steps on the narrow stairway. But Adrian's riposte stopped him in his tracks.

'It's hardly the hour for social calls, is it? But perhaps that's not what you had in mind.'

The doctor swung round on his heel, fists clenched. 'Damn you, you should know!' One hand shot out and grasped the lapel of the blue robe and at that moment Kate, who had been cowering in the bathroom, shivering with horror as she listened to the interchange, flung wide the door and stepped out on to the landing, her mass of hair falling out of its topknot, cheeks pink with fright, eyes huge and dark and accusing.

It seemed to Kate that Luke was about to hit the much smaller man — and as ever she leapt to the underdog's defence.

'You brute! Leave Adrian alone — ' She pushed between the two of them. 'Adrian, go back inside, I'll deal with Mr Harvey.' And when Adrian showed a reluctance to comply, 'Please, dear, don't worry about me, just go back in.'

Luke snorted with maddened fury. So this was the real Kate Cameron. No Cinderella after all, no little Goody Two Shoes. To think he had allowed himself to be so taken in, while all the time the wretched girl entertained men in her flat, allowed others liberties which he . . .

'Right, young woman!'

Into the bathroom Luke thrust Kate, pushed her against the wall, the moon's watery light illuminating his dark bulk while masking his twisted, furious features. Paralysed with disbelief, Kate could not move, her arms flung wide against the icy ceramic tiles, fingers sliding helplessly across the slippery, unyielding surfaces.

'No Luke — !'

This had never featured in the most technicolour of her dreams: an angry, bitter struggle in a freezing bathroom, Prince Charming's face a scornful, derisive, *unloving* mask in which his grey eyes glittered as if with frozen tears.

Just as suddenly the anger drained out of Luke. He relaxed his grip on her, stepped back, head averted. 'No, you're right — revenge is never sweet.' There was a long pause in which Kate could feel her own heart thudding in the cage of her ribs as though trying to escape its confines. She wrapped her shivering body more tightly in the damp towel, watching Luke as he turned to gaze sightlessly through the bathroom's frosted window.

'I came,' he said quietly, 'because I had to talk to you. I drove past, saw the light upstairs, took the risk that I did. And found you were already occupied.' He turned and began to move away, out of the room, out of the building — out of her life. As though hypnotised Kate followed. At the top of the stairs Luke paused briefly. 'I'm a proud man, Kate Cameron. I shan't bother you again, have no fear of that.'

He was disappearing now into the darkness of the stairwell, leaving her in the midst of a waking nightmare. But Kate could not find the words to call him back. The tears were flowing now, silently cascading down her frozen cheeks. Suddenly she found her voice and called to him. 'Go back to your wife then, Luke Harvey, and I hope she never finds out the sort of man you really are.'

But the only sound that came back to her was the echo of the front door as it slammed behind him, the growl of the engine as he started his car and drove away.

Back in the flat a goggling Joanna was trying to calm down Adrian, plying him with Horlicks and persuading him to get to bed. Indeed no, there was nothing serious between Luke Harvey and Kate. If anyone would know about that, she would.

'Whatever was the row about?' She followed Kate into her room, closing the door behind them so Adrian could not hear what they were saying. 'Do you realise he was all for packing his bag and leaving there and then? I've had the devil's own job to persuade him to get to bed. He obviously got the impression you'd something going with Mr Harvey — and I'm not sure I blame him in view of what's happened.'

Kate looked shattered. Dark rings like purple bruises shadowed her eyes. What on earth could she do to sort out such a muddle of misunderstanding? Adrian must be thinking she had deliberately misled him and that Mr

Harvey was in the habit of turning up on her doorstep at all hours; not to mention being closely acquainted with what she wore in the privacy of her bedroom! It was like some outlandish French farce — but not a bit funny. To tell the truth, Kate felt rather ill with the awfulness of everything; and knowing Luke believed she and Adrian were lovers — for some reason that was the worst of all. Even though he was married himself, it hurt unbelievably that he should believe her so deceitful, so uncaring, when if he only knew how she had to fight against the depth of her true feelings for him . . .

And that awful scene in the bathroom!

'Jo, how am I ever going to face Luke Harvey again? Yet I have to — on a professional level anyway. Please, Jo, tell me what I must do!'

Urgently Kate grabbed at her friend's wrist, but though Joanna was sympathetic there was no easy way out.

'Chin up, love, there's no way you

can avoid a senior registrar who's looking after patients on your own ward. Just tell yourself it'll all be forgotten this time next week. That's the way life goes. Now, let's get to bed and sleep on things.'

Kate supposed reluctantly that the other nurse was right, seeing she'd had much more experience of such matters. There was going to be no other choice but to hold her head high, not let Luke Harvey sense what it cost her to pretend.

8

It was dreadful next morning. Adrian's face was pale and set, and when tentatively Kate attempted to speak of what had happened, he shook his head.

'It's your life and none of my business, so don't let's talk about it. I hope we can still be friends.'

He drove away after breakfast, kissing her goodbye with an air of polite formality, shaking hands with Jo who was a pale shadow of her usual ebullient self.

When they were alone Joanna flung herself down at the table, her elbows resting in a litter of toast crumbs and dirty plates. Silently Kate poured two cups of strong black coffee and joined her. It was difficult to know what to say — so she said nothing.

Jo broke the silence first, tapping her cigarette end on the Formica surface.

'Well, Kate, love, a night to forget. I'm afraid you've lost yourself two fine fellas.'

Kate struck a match and lit the other girl's cigarette.

'Hold still, you've got the shakes this morning. Glad I shan't be on the end of your hypodermic.' Through a haze of smoke Jo stared at her friend with shrewd and sympathetic eyes. 'Not to worry,' she drawled in tones intended to be consoling. 'There's plenty more pebbles on the beach — and you've still got Dr Barnes on your trail. I know, we'll start all over again at the St Valentine's Ball. That's always a riot!'

'Heaven forbid!' Kate groaned audibly. 'I've had just about as much excitement as I can cope with.'

Jo grinned and stretched, cigarette ash powdering the front of her white towelling robe. She brushed it away carelessly, made a grimy mark on the fabric and swore. 'Sorry, kid. It's a pity about Adrian though — he's a nice boy, just your type.'

Shrugging, Kate acknowledged that yes, he was nice; but all the same, no hearts had been broken.

'If you say so. But I guess you were right about one thing after all, Kate. You're definitely not Mr Harvey's type — he's too much for you to handle. Who'd have guessed he'd got such a temper? . . . I never thought we'd get you out of that bathroom in one piece! Do you want to finish that piece of toast?'

Kate shook her head but continued to sit there, morosely watching Joanna munch her way through the remnants of Kate's breakfast.

'Course, he's *bound* to think of himself as God Almighty being a surgeon and with those looks,' Jo observed.

Surprisingly enough, Kate found herself biting back the urge to spring to Luke's defence, so busied herself instead with tidying away the breakfast things and getting on with the washing-up. Anything to keep her mind and hands occupied. Yet it wasn't typical of Jo to be critical about the medics; usually she was as ready as most of them to jump if a good-looking doctor so much as flicked his fingers.

'Everything okay with you and Tom?' asked Kate perceptively. 'You're not usually so down on the medical profession,' she added drily.

Jo grinned back at her, a touch ruefully. 'I'm feeling neglected, that's what's wrong with me. He's so tied up finishing that fellowship thesis . . . and here's you with guys fighting over you. No wonder I'm jealous.'

'You do exaggerate,' reproved Kate, blushing a little as she hung up the tea-towel to dry.

'All the same, I am sorry about Adrian. I could swear he was on the verge of doing the good old-fashioned, down-on-his-knees-type proposal. Then that great idiot had to turn up and blow the whole thing sky high.'

'Well,' insisted Kate stoutly, 'maybe he did us both a favour. I don't want to marry anyone. I'm a career nurse through and through.'

Jo shrugged, stubbing her cigarette out in the tin ashtray. 'If you say so. Now I have to fly, I'm going to be late as usual.'

'And I'm on again tonight. I shall be glad to get back to my old ladies and be rid of these troublesome men.'

* * *

Efficiently Nerys Cooper worked through the Kardex, giving Kate a succinct report on each and every patient. 'It's been reasonably quiet today. Mrs Daniels needs careful monitoring after that episode of bleeding. And we've got two new admissions in since Tuesday. Mrs Fox in the side ward is very confused — you'll see we've kept cot sides up.'

'What's she written up for, Staff?'

Cooper checked the records. 'Sparine injection intramuscularly every eight hours.' She handed over the keys to the drugs cupboard. 'I suppose you heard about Sister's accident?'

The day sister on F6 had inexplicably run her car off the road, heading homeward the previous day. Everyone was blaming it on fatigue, for Sister Lucas, unmarried and in her early fifties, was determined to carry on looking after her elderly invalid mother at home whatever the cost to herself in time and energy.

Staff Nurse Cooper appeared in no great hurry to go off duty.

'Is anyone visiting Sister Lucas?' asked Kate with concern.

Nerys collected her basket from behind the filing cabinet, folded her navy cardigan and put it on top of a box of sweets given to her by one of the patients. Kate pretended not to notice; it was frowned on to accept gifts from the ward.

'Well, I'm told the SNO's been, but maybe one of us ought to ring. I'll do that when I get home. Sister's okay apart from torn ligaments and bruises, she'll soon be back, knowing her.'

Jennings poked her rosy round face through the open door. 'Kettle's on. What about you, Staff?'

'You night nurses, you're all as bad as each other,' said Nerys Cooper good-humouredly. 'Cups of tea the minute you come on duty, out with the knitting and put your feet up!'

'Watch it, Staff!' Kate joined in the banter, typical between night and day staff. 'We shall be obliged to hold you hostage for the night to jog your failing memory. Be with you in five minutes, Jennings — I must pop round the ward and say hello to everyone.'

She took her time, strolling unhurriedly from bed to bed, stroking a frail hand here, plumping a pillow there.

'What lovely chrysanths, Mrs Lee — I can see your daughter's been in again today.'

'Have a chocolate, Nurse,' offered Mrs Lee reluctantly, well aware she'd been caught in the act.

A whole pound box, and most of them scoffed already. Really, Mrs Lee's daughter ought to know better since her obese mother was on that carefully regulated diet. Kate closed the box and slid it far into the back of the locker, feeling mean as she did so. 'Save the rest for tomorrow,' she suggested gently and moved on down the ward.

In the next bed Elspeth was sitting up, looking pretty in a soft blue angora jacket she'd knitted herself before arthritis had crippled her poor hands. She was leafing through a pile of magazines her visitors had left that afternoon.

'See this pattern here, Nurse? Suit you a treat that would.'

'Hmm, yes, I'm fond of red,' said Kate, considering.

'C'm here,' insisted Elspeth with a nod of her head; she was an inveterate gossip and loved to pry into the nurses' private lives. Not that she meant any harm, Kate knew; it just relieved the monotony.

'That boyfriend of yours — he hasn't been in lately. On his holidays is he?

Think you'd have gone with him.' She watched Kate slyly, waiting for her to give herself away with a blush.

'What boyfriend, Elspeth?' Kate frowned, genuinely puzzled.

'That one who comes in when we're all supposed to be asleep. Nice looking fellow, very healthy colour he's got. Now I like that in a doctor, gives you confidence. Who wants to be treated by someone who looks all wishy-washy?'

Kate's brow suddenly cleared. 'Oh, you must be talking about Mr Luke Harvey. He's not my boyfriend, Elspeth — don't go telling people that, will you? You've no idea how quickly gossip gets around in a hospital, worse than a forest fire! Anyway,' she added, 'it's the patients Mr Harvey comes to see, not me.'

Elspeth chuckled. 'You kidding, Nurse? He don't bother to come when you're not on, I can tell you.'

A pulse began to throb remorselessly in Kate's left temple. If the way she really felt about the man was obvious even to patients watching them together on the ward then, heaven help her, Luke himself must be aware he held her in the palm of his hand. No wonder he sensed she was giving him double messages; saying one thing while her physical self betrayed the attraction she was so determined to subdue. He must be fearfully amused at her predicament.

Still Elspeth was chirruping on like a demented robin. '*Luke*. Now that's what I call a nice name — Luke, Luke. I once read a book, you know, about a doctor called Luke. It might have been a religious book but I can't quite recall ... Anyways, the title was *Beloved Physician*. And now you've got a Beloved Physician of your own, Nurse — and he's called Luke too!'

Kate grabbed hold of Elspeth's toes through the coverlet and gave them a little shake. 'Sssh, now! I've told you he's not my boyfriend once and for all, you bad girl. Stop it now or I'll make your Horlicks all lumpy!'

With a giggle, Elspeth went back to

reading her magazines — but not before bestowing on the hapless Kate a broad wink suggestive of shared secrets. In spite of her apparent nonchalance, a knot of apprehension speared Kate in the diaphragm — though she put it down to two doughnuts with her tea. She forced herself to concentrate on the patients as she continued round the ward, to put her own problems right to the back of her mind.

One of the new admissions, a retired teacher with a lobar pneumonia and ulcerated legs, was fretting over her two cats. Kate tried to reassure the thin little woman with her sunken cheeks and general air of malnutrition, that the medical social worker would indeed be as good as her word and would see to it that the two vital men in her life, Henry and Boaz, were given their usual diet of fresh liver and fish.

'Tinned food just doesn't agree with them. I must get back to look after them as quickly as I can.'

Kate felt sad for the poor woman.

Those cats obviously ate far better than Miss Mason herself; but who could measure the love and affection they gave in return? In the meantime she lay propped high on pillows and chafed over her own physical weakness.

With a rattle of cups, a trolley loaded with hot milky drinks pulled up at the end of the bed. 'What would you like to drink, my dear?' shouted Student Nurse Khan, a wand-slim Asian who appeared to operate on the assumption that grey hairs automatically affected the hearing.

Miss Mason winced. 'I'm not deaf you know, Nurse,' she grumbled. 'What have you got?'

Unabashed, Nurse Khan counted them off on her long brown fingers. 'Horr-licks, Ovaltine, warr-m milk — or Bourrn-vita,' rolling her rs with relish.

Night Sister came bustling through the swing doors, nodded to Kate as she turned in to the ward office and picked up the phone. Kate hastened to join her.

'Soon as you're ready,' the senior

nurse was saying briskly into the receiver, 'we've a bed on F6.' She put the phone down again. 'Ah, Nurse Cameron, an emergency admission for you from Casualty, awaiting surgery when there's a theatre free.'

Kate nodded, immediately alert to the alteration in the night's routine. Only three staff — but somehow they would cope, as they always did.

'I want you to put her in the single room opposite Mrs Fox. Mrs Tucker is something of a special case — retired Matron of St Xavier's.' She named one of the country's foremost teaching hospitals. 'The night theatre porter will be bringing her up shortly and I don't have to remind you of the need for close observation until she goes up to theatre.'

'No, Sister,' replied Kate meekly. 'Not much point asking for an extra pair of hands, I suppose?'

Regretfully Sister shook her head. 'No, dear, I'm very sorry but you'll just have to cope. We're always struggling at this time of year as well you know. No need to send a nurse to theatre with the patient though, they'll have a spare junior. Oh, and tell your colleagues to watch their ps and qs; madam's a tartar of the old school. One of the porters has already had a rocket for clumsy handling of the stretcher!'

Judging by his disgruntled expression, it was the same grey-coated porter who wheeled Matron Tucker into the ward some ten minutes later. He thrust the case notes at Kate and guided the trolley into the room she indicated, where Nurse Khan was ready and waiting. The porter ran the trolley alongside the bed and together the three of them lifted the elderly woman with the utmost care, transferring her easily to the bed and returning the blankets from Casualty to the trolley. The patient, Kate noticed with a keen glance of appraisal, looked ashen, eyes sunk now with the ravages of pain, yet glittering with fever; skin cold and clammy with shock.

Intending to slip to the office for a glance at the case notes, Kate followed the porter outside into the ward passage.

'All this fuss over an eighty-year old woman!' he muttered callously.

Her back to the ward entrance, Kate's blood boiled at such lack of charity. 'God help *you* then when you're old and ill,' she snapped tersely. 'I dare say you'll find pain's as unbearable whether you're thirty or eighty!'

The surly expression on the man's face changed now to sheepishness and at the same moment Kate became aware of someone standing close behind her.

'Very well said!'

For a moment she hardly recognised him in theatre greens, his hair covered by his cap, mask dangling. Then the green-robed figure moved past her and into the room where the new admission lay awaiting surgery. Catching Kate's eye, Nurse Khan slipped out to help

Jennings in the main ward, while Kate stayed to assist Luke Harvey.

Matron Tucker opened her eyes wearily, obviously dreading the prospect of yet another examination. Something in Luke, however, told her that he was not someone who would succumb to a flare of out-dated intimidation. The look in his grey eyes, compassionate yet totally in control, comforted — Kate saw — more than a thousand assurances. Elspeth's words leapt unbidden to her mind. Luke, the beloved physician . . .

To her own surprise, Kate now found herself completely calm and cool. The sight of Luke Harvey, his presence there so close to her once again . . . having to face him after what had happened back at her flat! Why, she'd feared she'd behave like a gibbering idiot.

But it was as if each in their uniform was encased in a neutralising armour which would allow them to work calmly together, with mutual trust and respect, even perhaps to enjoy the professional side of their relationship.

Kate moved silently to Luke's side and handed him the brown manila folder. Rapidly his eyes perused the observations of the night Casualty Officer, bottom lip out-thrust in consideration of the implications for him as surgeon. His shadow loomed gigantic against the night-light, presiding over the drama and its three protagonists. Mrs Tucker lay quiet and still, eyes closed in resignation.

'Mrs Tucker,' he said in his calm and reassuring baritone, 'I shall need you to answer a few questions for me.'

Luke handed the folder back to Kate, who stood close by, ready to help when required.

With an effort the woman turned her head to look at them both.

'I don't want to examine you more than I can help. Please tell me what you can about your past medical history.'

Mrs Tucker's voice started off in a whispery trail but gradually grew stronger. She explained how she had

had trouble with her bowels over a number of years and been treated by her GP for diverticulosis, which had slowly developed into diverticulitis.

Kate knew this was a frequent complaint among elderly people whose diet was over-refined and contained too little roughage. In consequence, the bowel developed pockets of inflammation where scraps of food lodged and decayed, causing the bouts of feverish tummy pains which Mrs Tucker was describing now to Luke and which her doctor had been able to treat with antibiotics.

'How often has this happened? Once, twice, three or four times?'

'Oh no,' sighed the sick woman. She had suffered with infected diverticulae on at least ten occasions.

'And what happened earlier today?'

Kate pushed a chair behind Luke, knowing he must have been standing in theatre for some hours, bending that muscular height over the operating table. He sat down automatically, relieved to be off his feet even momentarily, absorbed in what Mrs Tucker was telling him.

'I've had the usual pains, been feeling feverish and unwell over the last forty-eight hours. Then about five hours ago I began to feel very nauseous, noticed I had a rapid pulse and a raised temperature. Also my stomach was rock hard and tender.'

Kate listened carefully too. Here was an articulate and intelligent lady with considerable experience herself of what could go wrong with the human body. She must have a pretty good idea of what was on the cards — even if twenty years had passed since she last worked in a hospital. The ex-matron had had the good sense to ring for an ambulance and have herself brought direct to Accident and Emergency without further delay, anticipating there must be some sort of obstruction in the colon.

Luke's expression was firmly sympathetic. 'I'm going to examine you now,' he warned. 'I shall be as gentle as I can but this is bound to be uncomfortable.'

Mrs Tucker obviously intended to comply with whatever Luke suggested, though it had been a different scene earlier, from what Kate had heard. 'I quite appreciate that,' she replied with frail dignity, and her old hands moved to turn back the sheets for him. Kate went to help her, folding back the blankets and tucking the hospital gown out of the way. She could only too easily imagine what Mrs Tucker was going through; the indignity of having to submit to the weaknesses of your own body after a lifetime of caring for others. Nurses were notoriously impatient patients!

Luke was concentrating now, listening for bowel sounds, stethoscope applied to the rigid abdomen. He glanced at Kate and shook his head with a slight frown. A bad sign, the look signified. Then he noted how the lightest pressure to the stomach brought beads of perspiration to Mrs Tucker's haggard brow, which Kate wiped gently away with a cool flannel.

'I'm testing now for rebound tenderness,' Luke explained in a low murmur. The patient nodded and closed her eyes bravely. Kate watched as the lean brown hands expertly applied a slow, firm pressure on the abdomen, noted the way Luke's eagle eyes estimated, after a quick release of that pressure, how soon the woman's stomach regained its rock-hard convexity. Mrs Tucker was a hefty and well-preserved woman for her years.

Again Kate wiped the sweat from the furrowed white forehead. It looked as if the bowel had burst and Mrs Tucker was very ill indeed.

In the office Luke explained his findings.

'This is a case of diverticulitis — with a perforation which has given rise to peritonitis. Bowel sounds are non-existent. We must operate as soon as possible. Now, I've another emergency op scheduled for nine-thirty but we should be ready for Mrs Tucker by eleven. In the meantime you'll monitor her closely of course, pulse and BP etc.'

He glanced at his wrist, suddenly recollected he was not wearing a watch and peered at the fob watch Kate hastily showed him. Then he looked down at the nurse standing there before him, her dark eyes reflecting concern for his punishing schedule, mingled with a touching faith and admiration and something which might be interpreted as apologetic regret.

Momentarily a muscle flickered in his lean cheek, but the eyes, glazed now with fatigue, regarded Kate with a new and clinical detachment.

As he left the ward, Kate stood rooted silent in misery. After all, Joanna was right; any feeling there now was entirely her own.

By one-fifteen Luke had cleared the obstruction and washed Mrs Tucker's insides clear. Deftly he put in the final suture and stood back while the wound was swabbed dry and strapping secured over a drainage tube. On the rack hung a row of blood-stained sponges. The anaesthetist injected pethidine to keep Mrs Tucker comfortable and pain-free over the next critical hours, and Luke ordered antibiotics to be administered.

A nurse passed behind him and untied the neck of his theatre gown. He flung his bloodied rubber gloves into the bin, his gear into the hamper and sank into a chair in the changing room to down with gratitude the steaming coffee one of the nurses brought to him.

He thought longingly of bed. And then, frowning, of Nurse Cameron who would be specialling his patient.

To hell with the girl. He was just too weary to care what she did with her life.

Luke had got over the shock of finding his assumptions about Kate Cameron were quite wrong; that she was, after all, a modern girl in spite of the handicap of her father's profession. All the same, he knew he would never again see her in quite the same light . . .

How on earth had she found out

about Lydia? For that accusation flung at him as he left her flat showed that Nurse Cameron, for her own good reasons, had been doing some research into his private affairs.

Luke lit a cigarette and lounged back in the easy chair, deep in reflection. It might be interesting to see her reactions when presented with the truth. Yes, it would mean gouging into old wounds to open up a past he would prefer forgotten, but she would be better equipped to understand the need for such secrecy that day he had smuggled her into Professor Hall's home.

That bedside photo — of course! She would have seen that; but was it really sufficient evidence to make her so determinedly proper with him?

Yes, considered Luke, running a hand through his short curls, then grinding the stub of his cigarette into a nearby ashtray. Pictured in morning dress with a laughing bride on one's arm; yes, it was pretty conclusive evidence.

He drained his cup and rose, stretching to his full height. The time would come when he could set her conscience at rest; he looked forward to that. But now for that cell they called the duty officer's bed-sit.

* * *

Kate regarded her patient with a sense of unease, checking the time with her fob watch. Two hours since Mrs Tucker had come back from theatre. They had monitored her pulse and blood pressure as ordered — yet Kate felt unhappy about the charts. She studied them yet again. Ninety systolic over forty diastolic. Surely that blood pressure reading was far too low, the heartbeat irregular and fibrillating . . .

The drip continued to feed antibiotics and pethidine into the patient's blood stream. Kate watched its monotonous regularity. Ought she to speed the drip a little? Should Mr Harvey be informed? No, it would be unthinkable to disturb his night's sleep just to allay her own misgivings. Besides, she could not bring herself to bother him — why, her heart pounded at the very idea . . .

But that's just a personal thing, an insistent voice from within began to argue. Just because you have to psych yourself up to face him! You have just as great a duty towards this patient as you had to Kevin Cash. Blow inconveniencing the surgeon! It's his job to come, and yours to haul him out of bed if his patient needs to be seen. Get on with it — he can only bite your head off!

Before her courage could desert her, Kate marched to the office phone, checked the call numbers of the doctors on the duty list and began to dial. Her fingers trembled but she kept going — nurse on duty, not Kate Cameron. Keep it strictly impersonal.

'Yes?' The voice that answered sent chills down Kate's spine.

'Nurse Cameron on F6,' she said tightly. 'I'm concerned about your patient Mrs Tucker — the obstruction.'

'What's happening?' Luke sounded wide awake.

'I'd be grateful if you'd take a look at her please. Her pulse is irregular and her BP is very low. She appears to be deteriorating.'

'I'll be right over,' came the unhurried reply. There was a click as the receiver was replaced and Kate found herself hanging on to silence. He was coming. Kate swallowed hard and forced her shoulders back. A quick look in the office mirror showed her cap in place, her hair less tidy than she would have wished; face pale, eyes huge and defiant — chin weak and trembling! She ground her jaws together and agonised over the tension in her spine, forcing herself to remember she had managed to face him earlier with some semblance of calm. Why should it be any different this time — so long as she knew she was in the right?

In Mrs Tucker's room Kate checked all her observations. No improvement; if anything a further deterioration.

Luke came in noiselessly and under her long lashes Kate saw he was wearing narrow black cords and T-shirt pulled on hastily beneath his white coat. Far from looking tired, he exuded strength and animal magnetism — along with that inevitable air of assured authority. Even so, Kate was suddenly aware that the golden tan was fading, the cropped curls were longer now, forming tendrils at the collar of his coat. All this registered in her mind in the space of seconds as she lowered her gaze to avoid direct contact with those cobra-grey eyes.

In silence Luke worked over the patient, double-checking the readings Kate had filled in so neatly on the charts, reaching across to adjust the drip which controlled the fluid input to the veins of Mrs Tucker's left arm.

Then he spoke — an abrupt undertone of command.

Kate nodded silently and slipped from the room, to return within seconds with the two bricks he had asked for — ordinary builders' bricks. Together they lifted the foot of the hospital bed so that the bricks rested one beneath each castor. Mrs Tucker lay now with her head lower than her feet by an angle of fifteen degrees, which would help increase the flow of blood to her brain.

For a few seconds longer Luke remained at the bedside, intent in his observation of the patient. Then he turned at last to Kate, who stood mutely by, her eyes reflecting so much more than straightforward professional concern . . .

Involuntarily Luke made a move towards her — then changed his mind for some reason and concentrated on the vigorous washing of his hands at the basin. 'She's doing well,' he murmured, satisfied. 'I've speeded up the drip so there's increased fluid in her circulation. Her cardiac output will soon rise — you'll find within the hour you'll see a much improved blood pressure now that we've adjusted the bed.'

He placed a firm hand in the small of Kate's back and guided her in the direction of the office where they could talk without disturbing the sleeping patients.

Relief ran through her veins — warm, liquid pleasure stemming from the comforting sense of his touch upon her, approval once more in his voice . . .

'I am sorry,' she said with regret. 'I hated to disturb you.'

'You were quite right to call me — it's what I'm here for. What you were not aware of is that pethidine can have the effect of lowering the blood pressure, which could easily mislead the nurse into thinking the patient may be becoming shocked due to blood loss, cardiac failure — or even septicaemia. Now we've elevated her feet and speeded up that drip, Mrs Tucker's condition will stabilise. Apart from some atrial fibrillation she's doing well and this is just a temporary set-back. All the same, one doesn't take risks with an elderly patient who has undergone a hefty anaesthetic.'

His words produced in Kate a glowing sense of satisfaction. How it helped to work with a surgeon prepared to take the trouble to explain what was happening, instead of just assuming that the nurse's interest began and ended with bedpans and thermometers. Mr Harvey was *not* furious at being dragged out of bed — and Mrs Tucker was on the mend.

Kate heaved a gusty sigh. 'Thank you. Thank you very much indeed.'

'I'll see you tomorrow,' Luke promised softly. 'Or do I mean tonight? Ah well — '

Their eyes caught and held with a new and mutual respect. Then out of the blue the bleeper in Luke's pocket shrilled its urgent call, destroying all the promise of that moment.

'Yes?' rapped Luke into the office phone. 'A private call — at *this* hour! From *where?*' There was a short pause while he listened intently and Kate moved uncertainly to the door. She ought to escort him from the ward, but if he was receiving a personal call it would be more tactful to wait in the passage.

'Do you realise what time it is over here?' The surgeon's voice was alert with tension and surprise. 'Is something wrong?'

Kate's skin was still prickling with resentment at such an ill-timed interruption of what might have been a chance for reconciliation. Through the closed door she could hear Luke's affectionate throaty chuckle. 'My dear Harry,' he was saying, 'I can always rely on you to do the unexpected.'

Kate bit her lip hard, trying not to eavesdrop but helpless with curiosity.

'The job's tremendous — it's the natives,' another ironical chuckle, 'who can be hard to handle.' Then, 'I am — I can — I most certainly shall . . . Take care of yourself.'

Luke's younger brother no doubt, decided Kate as she heard the click of the receiver being replaced, her mind's eye full of the image of a younger, sweeter, but undoubtedly more *thoughtless* version of Luke. Fancy ringing at such a strange hour!

9

'Kate! I enjoyed that almost as much as your delicious cooking. What's your verdict?' Dr Barnes hauled himself to his feet, crossed the sitting-room to switch off the video recorder, then joined Kate once more, sinking back into the sumptuous velvet cushions. He flung an arm about Kate who snuggled, fearless as a kitten, up to his side.

'I think,' she pronounced, 'that was the best idea we've had. Supper here at your flat and a quiet night in, watching a decent film. Smashing.'

Hayden Barnes tightened his arm about her in an affectionate squeeze. 'My little reformer! I know you're not really keen on those smart nightclubs and restaurants I drag you off to . . . '

'We-ell, if I'm strictly honest — though it's exciting as an occasional treat to be taken somewhere super and posh . . . '

'Oh, don't start sparing my feelings *now*, young lady — it's never deterred you in the past!'

A sheepish grin spread over Kate's calm, relaxed features. They were both well aware of what the doctor referred to — that cold January day on Casualty. And that had been the first of many disagreements when Kate stoutly held her own against the opinionated Hayden Barnes. Particularly as she had set out to reform his drinking habits. Her mission in life, they both called it, but Kate was in deadly earnest even if the doctor regarded her efforts with affectionate tolerance.

'I do like coming to your flat, Hayden dear — it's so luxuriously cosy. And that fabulous kitchen is a dream come true.'

'You know you can always move in . . . '

Kate immediately sat up and smoothed her skirt over her knees. 'Let's not go into all that again, please. We've sorted

261

out our relationship so let's stick to it. You can have as many lady friends as you like and I promise not to be jealous. Just so long as we continue to enjoy each other's company as friends and I can keep an eye on you.'

'It's a most unromantic relationship,' complained Hayden with a wry grin. 'And you sound dreadfully pompous for such a snippet.'

'This is no laughing matter,' Kate insisted seriously, regarding her companion with a frown. 'You're a brilliant man. I regard it as my mission to preserve your career from the demon drink . . . '

'Look at my hands — rock steady!'

'Yes, dear, they are now. But you mustn't take risks with the talents God has given you.'

Hayden snorted at this, telling her she was beginning to *sound* like a missionary. 'If you start looking like one,' he warned, laughing into the pretty face watching him with such concern, 'then I'm warning you you've had your chance. I only surround myself with beautiful women.'

He pulled her down for a kiss to which Kate responded gently, no longer afraid of the doctor's reputation, for she trusted him now with liking and respect. Not so long ago it had been very different . . .

'What you need is a good wife,' she mused when he released her. 'Someone to keep you in order. I shall look out for the right person. Have you met my friend Joanna?' she asked suddenly.

'That curly blonde? She's been around too much for my liking, dated every medic in the place.'

'Not that she'd be interested,' mused Kate. 'She's been going out with Tom for so long now I shouldn't be surprised . . . All the same, you'd be far better suited with someone used to hospital life than these glamorous actresses and models you go about with. Someone with a bit of character who can stand up to you and yet be understanding about your work and the demands it puts upon you. You wouldn't need to turn to the bottle for comfort then. Just look at the time — and you're operating at eight-thirty! I'm going to make you some coffee and then you can run me home.'

Kate disappeared into the kitchen, leaving Hayden to watch the late news on television. While she waited for the kettle to boil she entertained herself thinking of a suitable wife for him. Her thoughts drifted into considerations of how wrong you could be about people — how much she had disliked him in the early days; how fond she was of him now. But all the same, he was not the man she could marry.

'Have you ever met Luke Harvey's wife?' she asked casually enough as she poured steaming coffee into Hayden's delicate porcelain cups. 'He behaves as though she doesn't exist — yet I'm told he's married to someone very beautiful.'

'Luke Harvey's wife is dead,' came the bald reply, Hayden's eyes never leaving the flickering screen as his hand reached steadily for the proffered cup. 'She died a year or so after they were married. Her father was Maurice Hall, the Professor. Want a brandy before you go?'

'I do not — and neither do you.' Sick with sadness for the lovely bride enshrined in that exquisite room she had peeped into, and no less for Luke Harvey himself, Kate crouched by Hayden's feet on the carpet. All the implications of Luke's behaviour gradually dawned upon her and Kate was filled with shame and self-hatred at her own part in adding to his difficulties.

'You can switch that thing off now, Kate. Hey, wake up! You look miles away.'

'I was thinking about Mr Harvey's wife. Did you know her?'

He shook his head. 'Harvey spent the past few years out in Kenya working in a mission hospital. Trying to escape from reality, I should guess.'

'Ah, so that's why he's still so

sun-tanned. We all wondered about that. But I can't really see him as a missionary all the same . . . '

Hayden laughed dryly. 'I don't imagine Harvey's concern was for the spiritual welfare of the natives. He was purely interested in their medical needs. Friends of his from medical school days, a married couple, trained doctors both of them, were already out there. Then the husband got killed in a jeep accident and Luke felt bound to stay longer than he had intended.'

'I wonder what brought him back to England?'

'I know why I'd come back,' observed Hayden, his shrewd eyes on the girl crouched tensely beside his chair. 'Boredom, loneliness, lack of career opportunities. I should imagine he's over the worst. Time's a great healer, so they say, and he's certainly kept up his skills. In fact he's a remarkably experienced surgeon.'

Next day Kate was up determinedly early, even though she was still in the middle of her days off. She had no thoughts of going home, this late February morning, but headed straight for the hospital. What she must do was of vital importance, too vital to leave to some chance opportunity. She would seek out Luke Harvey, avoid him not a moment longer. He had wanted to talk to her at length, for whatever reason; that he had been unable to do so was entirely her fault and she blamed herself bitterly for her prim misunderstanding.

People had told her he must be attracted. Now Kate asked herself why that should not be, more confident now that Hayden Barnes made no secret of *his* liking for her. She was kind and caring and loving — and her face didn't seem to frighten the horses — so why not she, when she knew she could let herself love Luke Harvey more than any other woman ever should. And she longed to tell him so, assured now of the integrity of such a fine and admirable man.

But though Luke's car was there in the forecourt, the surgeon was nowhere to be found. Gradually the core of excitement which had buoyed her along dissolved into doubts and uncertainty. Kate no longer felt so sure that her purpose would be well received. In her heart she had built Luke Harvey up into some sorrowful paragon, but the truth was that he had a very teasing style when he chose and was master of the hurtful put-down. She could well be about to make the most awful fool of herself, Kate suddenly realised.

As a last try she had a word with the head porter. 'Mr Harvey?' he said. 'Now let's see — he's escorting a visitor, a Dr Crisp. They've gone across to the university campus to take a look at the medical school.'

'Thanks, George,' Kate turned away with a sigh of mingled relief and disappointment, her intention thwarted after all. She had hoped to get her apologies over while they were still relatively unpremeditated, before second thoughts could make her nervous. Now it would be easy to persuade herself she should leave well alone.

Immersed in her own problems, she bumped unseeingly into someone and found herself apologising to a beaming Roz.

'Haven't seen you since you've been on nights, Kate! Look, it's time for elevenses — come and have a coffee.'

It was while they were swapping gossip in the staff dining-room that Luke and the visiting doctor walked in. With her new knowledge of him, Kate's heart bounded against the confines of her ribcage and her throat went dry with emotion. That's the man I love, she wanted to confess to Roz — but of course, such an admission was impossible. Luke, in an immaculate midnight-blue suit, looked superb. He towered over the petite woman at his side.

'And to think we all thought it would be *you* capturing the luscious Mr

Harvey,' exclaimed Roz. 'Take a look at that!'

'*That* happens to be a visiting doctor.' There was more than a touch of indignation in Kate's voice — George had not mentioned a *lady* doctor.

'That's as maybe,' asserted Roz, giving the couple a shrewd, experienced once-over. 'But they're far from strangers. Just see the way they look at each other, the way she's touching his arm.'

With immense and painful curiosity, Kate observed the pair, disapproving immediately of all she saw; the ridiculously high heels of expensive shoes drawing attention to shapely legs any woman would be proud of; the curvy, well-fleshed figure in a clinging beige suit; the handsome, carefully made-up face, animated beneath a brunette elfin hair-cut lightly streaked with premature grey. The woman must be in her thirties, but how she stood out from the crowd. Such a feminine creature bearing that masculine aura of confident authority; what Kate defined as the 'whatever happens I can cope' syndrome peculiar to the medical profession.

The doctor was sweeping the unfamiliar dining-room with shrewd, intelligent eyes, scouring her surroundings with an assured, confident gaze.

Luke said something to her, then rose and went behind her chair, helping Dr Crisp out of her jacket, which came off to reveal a soft white silk shirt cut like a man's, emphasising and flattering the tanned olive tones of her smooth complexion.

Immediately Kate's brain began to computerise snippets of information, matching them to the scene she was observing. The lady doctor from Africa — the ungodly hour of that phone call which Luke had taken with an air of stunned surprise ... Well, this was certainly not brother Harry.

'Mark my words,' Roz was saying with lugubrious satisfaction, 'those two have been lovers. I'm never wrong about things like that. Anyway, we all knew Luke Harvey must have a past.'

'But, Roz, it's not like that at all,' protested Kate unhappily, reluctant, yet longing to reveal what she had discovered. 'Mr Harvey's a very fine man, one of the best surgeons I've ever worked with.'

'So — he's human, isn't he? And he can't be on duty *all* the time . . . '

Luke was lighting her cigarette now and the woman's fingers had closed over his, keeping his hand and the flame steady, their eyes intimately tangled.

'I have to go now,' said Kate hurriedly, desperate to get away. The exit route lay past their table.

'Nurse Cameron,' called Luke as she rushed by, eyes averted. 'The porters said you were looking for me.'

Kate was obliged now to stop and face them both. 'I see you are busy, Mr Harvey — it was nothing urgent.'

Luke looked surprised at the idea that Kate should want to see him at all, as well he might. 'Another time then,' he suggested pleasantly, and Kate could have sworn he had picked up the vibrations of mutual dislike which flowed between the two women, if the amusement in his lazy eyes was anything to go by.

Kate faced their scrutiny with cool dignity, then on trembling legs fled back to the security of her flat.

But that was not to be the last of the matter. It was Hayden who confirmed her suspicions. He and Luke had been operating together to patch up a young child savaged by an Alsatian. Afterwards in the surgeons' rest room Luke had mentioned that he and the Professor had a visitor staying with them, a Dr Harriet Crisp, the woman with whom he had worked out in Africa. For some extraordinary reason which Kate could not fathom, Luke had suggested they might make up a foursome.

The evening proved as dreadful as Kate had feared. Harriet Crisp looked a million dollars, her animation and petite but curvaceous figure apparently captivating both men. She had a strong and confident personality coupled with what Kate felt was a rather unfeminine style of speech and humour — but that, she realised, was what came of being a woman in a man's world. Kate felt overshadowed and colourless by comparison. She sat quietly, excluded from the conversation for much of the time since Harriet made no attempt to draw her into things. The best part was listening to Luke holding forth on Africa, which he clearly loved, gleaning more about him from the anecdotes he told of times he and his doctor friends had shared together. It was easy to see that he and 'Harry', as Luke called her, had been so much more to each other than just friends after her husband had died, each in need of mutual consolation.

From time to time Kate sensed Luke's eyes upon her, a quizzical, unfathomable expression in their grey, brooding depths. Once he intercepted the little shake of the head she gave Hayden when he picked up the wine bottle to refill his empty glass. Hayden grinned, winked complicitly and put the bottle down again untouched, acknowledging her answering private smile.

All the way home she had to sit trapped in the Porsche, listening to Hayden raving on about Dr Crisp.

'If you're so smitten why don't you ask her out then? I don't own you — and I don't suppose Luke Harvey claims to own her, either.'

'Aha!' countered Hayden. 'But that doesn't mean he wants to share. After all, you and I aren't lovers.'

Kate's heart sank to her shoes; so Hayden thought what Roz thought. 'I expect they'll get married,' she said gloomily. 'I got the impression she's thinking of putting in for that gynae SHO job when it comes up.'

'Still, I might try my luck there, see if I can pinch her off him.'

Great! thought Kate. That's the last

man in my life preparing to walk out on me. Treating herself to a little tantrum of pique, she refused to kiss Hayden goodnight and slammed the door of his precious car, knowing how that would rile him.

10

At some point Kate supposed she *must* have fallen asleep, but after that evening of wining and dining with Luke and his Harriet, and Hayden Barnes, she tossed and turned and tormented herself. Her head throbbed with the realisation that for a few exhilarating, irrational hours since the discovery that he was not, after all, that most forbidden of species, a married man, she had been so foolish as to imagine there could be a chance of winning Luke's love.

Now with Harriet's arrival on the scene the bubble had burst. Luke would very soon marry again, for Harriet had made clear her intention to stay now she had come home. Luke must have been very persuasive.

For the next week he failed to put in any appearances when Kate was working and a junior registrar made his rounds instead. Kate guessed Mr Harvey was taking some time off to escort Harriet during her stay. It did no good to wallow in self-pity or allow jealousy to rear its ugly head — and Kate was no slouch when it came to self-denial. She felt off-colour and depressed but put it down to the time of year, even succeeding with her generous spirit to feel sorry for Dr Crisp, who had left behind such sunny climes and must face the end of the British winter.

With her last night on, Kate determined to rush home to the vicarage the very next day and bury herself in domesticity — beat the carpets, scrub the floors, forget Luke Harvey even existed.

Meanwhile, life on F6 continued as usual with its never-ending routine, though Jennings was convinced Kate was going down with one of those flu viruses, she was so silent and pale.

Together they had almost finished the bed-round. The trolley was trundled along to the last bed where Ethel Lee was waiting like a great white whale to be rubbed and powdered and made comfy for the night.

'We'll rub your back now, Mrs Lee. Put your right arm round my waist, sweetheart, and try to roll yourself towards me so Nurse can get at you. That's the way, my love — that's grand, you really are trying to help us tonight.' Red in the face with exertion, Jennings heaved eighteen solid stone of humanity on to her side so that Mrs Lee's back could be rubbed with surgical spirit to stave off bedsores. 'Hurry up, Kate,' she puffed, 'or you'll have to pick me and Mrs Lee off the floor!'

At that Mrs Lee relaxed her small efforts with a croak of alarm and fell back again on to the heap of pillows. She'd no intention of tumbling out of that high iron bed; she *knew* those nurses were not to be trusted, such slips of things they were. That Nurse Cameron, why a puff of wind could whirl her away. It wasn't good to be so tall and skinny; a man liked a real armful — and a patient liked to feel the nurses had a bit of brawn and muscle. Then they wouldn't make such a fuss about you being on the plump side. One fat fist closed secretively about the boiled sweetie that had fallen down into the bed; they wouldn't get their fingers on that!

Kate was searching the trolley now, picking up piles of night-dresses and sheets with a puzzled expression on her gentle face. She must be cracking up after all — she distinctly remembered putting that jar of waterproof cream on the trolley, right next to the bowl of soapy water . . .

Just then Nurse Khan breezed up. 'You wanting this?' She held out the missing jar. 'Matron Tucker demanded her back be rubbed this instant, so I borrowed the zinc cream.'

Kate grinned at her good-humouredly. 'Thought for a moment I was losing my grip. Would you mind taking over here for me while I get on with medicines? If you let me have that torn sheet, Jennings, I'll pop it in the mending hamper before it gets forgotten.'

The linen cupboard was a smallish dark room with no outside windows, sandwiched as it was behind the kitchen and the sluice. Racks of wooden shelving held all the ward linen and clothes. A couple of empty trolleys stood idle and a big hamper lay just inside the door, marked clearly with the label 'Mending Room — torn linen *must* be folded.'

With her toe, Kate raised the lid and dropped the sheet inside with one deft movement. She didn't bother to switch on the light for there was just enough from the corridor for her to see and reach the wicker hamper.

When the figure loomed up within the depths of the linen room Kate's first instinct was to scream out loud. Reeling back against the door frame, she clapped a hand to her mouth to stifle the cry. All those stories she had heard of crazed drug addicts secreting themselves on wards to steal the keys to the dangerous drugs cupboard! Her fingers closed grimly over the keys in her apron pocket.

'Kate!' came an urgent whisper. 'Kate, is it really you?'

Out of the gloom stepped a narrow figure in jeans and donkey jacket, blonde pony-tail drooping damply, cheeks flushed with cold, soaking, filthy trainers on the sore young feet.

Scarcely able to credit what she was seeing, Kate peered uncertainly into the darkness. 'Vicky?' She reached out an unsteady hand to reassure herself of the solidity of the shape which rushed now into her outstretched arms and, after a few moments of snivelling, pulled away.

'Vicky, darling, you're soaked!'

From that momentary lapse into dependence Vicky had recovered a spark of defiance. 'Dare say,' she agreed with exaggerated unconcern. 'It's snowing a blizzard out there. I hitched to the city and then walked to the hospital. My feet are sopping.'

It was she who pulled the door to

and switched on the light so the two of them were out of sight and earshot. Hitching herself on to a trolley, she pulled off shoe and sock to reveal mottled blue-red toes beneath.

Immediately Kate grabbed hold of a towel and began to massage those poor cold feet back to life with her own warm hands, still shocked to find her younger sister there on the ward when she should have been safely tucked up in bed in the school dorm.

'I've run away,' announced Vicky, somewhat superfluously.

'I had noticed,' replied her sister dryly.

Vicky tossed her straggling tail of hair with a defiant gesture. Her Cupid's bow mouth pursed into a sulky pout as she challenged Kate with huge cornflower eyes. She really was growing stunningly pretty; but what a night of all nights for such an exploit. And what on earth was Kate to do about it? Nothing before morning, that was definite. Somehow

Vicky must be concealed on the ward for the rest of the night.

For one wild moment Kate considered disguising her little sister in a flannelette nightdress and popping her into an empty bed — if only they had one to spare! She *must* be persuaded to return to boarding school; those A levels were vital. Vicky must be made to see sense . . .

'Thank the Lord it's my last night on. As for Luke — ' she shrugged despondently. It would be better if she never saw him again.

Vicky's eyebrows raised in two beautifully-plucked arches. 'Luke who?' she enquired nosily, knowing full well her sister was quite unaware of having spoken her thoughts aloud.

Kate chose to ignore this. 'Wait in here and I'll bring you a warm drink. There may even be an egg or two in the fridge and some cake left over from tea. Don't you dare come out of here.' She must warn the other nurses before they came charging in to restock the trolleys and got the fright of their lives.

Switching off the light before she opened the door a cautious inch or so, Kate surveyed the corridor — and found herself gazing at an expanse of white cotton stretched across a broad and brooding back. 'Oh no!' she wailed as that back whirled about to face her, shutting the door fast and stepping back, knuckles pressed to her mouth. Had she been spotted?

Light flooded in from the corridor and there stood Mr Harvey on the threshold, glowering down at her.

'Hell's teeth, woman,' he growled in irritation. 'Are you playing games with me again? I'm getting rather tired of it. In fact I think I'll have to come in there and punish you. I know a few games that can be played in linen cupboards . . . '

'Luke — wait!'

Something in Kate's horrified expression made him pause and glance into the darkness behind her. A hand reached across her shoulder and snapped on the light again. Vicky was illuminated, sitting there on the trolley, swinging her legs prettily. She sprang down and stood there in clinging sweater and jeans, thoroughly enjoying the way those hooded cobra eyes snaked interestedly over her, making no effort to hide the admiration in her own.

That was some little scene she'd almost witnessed between her sister and this hunk of a doctor who obviously knew Kate rather well . . .

'Do join us,' she suggested mockingly, with all the poise and sophistication her big sister lacked. 'Come in and close the door. It's getting very interesting in here.' Her blue eyes sparkled invitingly at Luke and Kate, to her chagrin, was once more deeply aware of her own deficiencies in the age-old art of flirtation. Her sister was obviously intrigued by the charismatic Luke Harvey — who could blame her? And for his part Luke had every appearance of being equally fascinated by her little sister. After all, here was a blonde version of Kate herself — with bags of personality and brain in the one package. Sixteen going on twenty-six, considered Kate ruefully. And not an inhibition or scruple in her pert little head.

Halting over the introductions, Kate explained Vicky's predicament and Luke listened to her story, nodding thoughtfully, eyes fixed the while on the youngster's glowingly pretty face.

He reached out to a peg on the back of the door, tossing across to Vicky the yellow uniform dress of a nursing auxiliary left there by one of the day staff, and with it the winged white cap.

'Put this on,' he was saying. 'You may as well find out how the other half earn their livings. It may even give you a taste for medicine instead of Classics — but be sure you keep out of Night Sister's way.'

Vicky's complicit chuckle of delight brought Kate back to her senses with a jolt. 'She can't do that!'

'I don't see why not,' argued Luke calmly. 'Now just you pop along, Kate, and see to the medicines while I have a little chat with your sister. Seems to me she could do with some objective advice.'

Kate gulped at the vision of bra and pants and smoothly gleaming limbs which Vicky was displaying so nonchalantly as she slipped out of her damp clothes and into the yellow dress. Really, the last thing she wanted to do was to leave Luke in there alone with her naughty little sister; and it showed all over her expressive face!

Luke grinned mockingly down at her. 'Off you go.' With a gentle shove he encouraged her out into the corridor where, with a little spurt of anger, Kate flounced away to unlock the drugs cupboard and see to the patients' medication.

Unsure whether she was angry with Luke or herself, Kate spoke little when she accompanied the doctor on his swift late round to check up on Professor Hall's own cases, and in particular Mrs Tucker. Politely but coolly she accompanied Luke to the door of the ward.

'Cheer up!' admonished the surgeon unromantically. 'I've had a very useful chat with your charming sister and she's agreed to be a good girl and go back to school tomorrow.'

He laughed at the astonishment which filled those huge dark eyes turned up to him in disbelief. 'I'll run you both there after lunch; afraid I can't make it earlier — there's a departmental meeting in the morning. Pick you up at your flat about two.'

He turned to leave, then looked back at Kate to suggest she ring the headmistress in the morning and let her know Vicky was safe. With his knuckles he jostled her stiff cheek — another totally unromatic gesture, she mused dejectedly, from the one man she hopelessly loved.

'Thank you very much,' she managed dispiritedly, struggling to inject genuine gratitude into her voice. 'It really is kind of you to help us . . .'

'You look washed out,' he said sympathetically. 'Poor old thing.' With that he was gone and the swing doors rocked under the impact of his exit.

★ ★ ★

Turning up the sound, Kate listened anxiously to the weather bulletin on the radio. More snow was predicted. You only had to look out of the flat window to see the leaden skies and the heavy spread of snow over roofs and back gardens. What the roads must be like she dreaded to think. It was going to be an awful nuisance for Luke, having to abandon Harriet to her own devices and lumber himself with a drive into the wilds of Shropshire.

Kate made some coffee and filled a vacuum flask to take on the journey, poured a fresh cup for herself and Vicky and went to wake her sister.

By the time Luke arrived they were both ready. Vicky's clothes had been dried and properly aired; Kate was wearing her black cords with a creamy Shetland polo-necked sweater, her hair twisted up into a glossy knot on the crown of her head, shiny red mac over one arm.

Luke turned to Vicky with a look of approval, his head swivelling back towards Kate, comparing dark and blonde versions on a similar theme. He was obviously intrigued by the sight of them together. 'Have you managed to get some sleep?'

'I've slept like a top.' Vicky smiled winningly up at him, her thick blonde hair loose now about her shoulders, freshly washed and gleaming. She looked the picture of health and happiness, so that it was hard to understand why only the day before she could have been sufficiently depressed, or bored, to be on the run from boarding school. 'Kate,' she pointed out, 'hasn't managed to get to bed at all. She must be worn out, poor thing!'

'In that case Kate must sleep on the back seat while you ride up front with me and tell me all about yourself.'

With Vicky ensconced beside the driver, Kate had no choice but to comply. A warm plaid rug was wrapped comfortingly around her and her sister brought out a cushion from the flat to put under her head. In truth, Kate was grateful for the chance to rest and the movement of the car soon lulled her, like a child, fast asleep.

Thus she knew little of the journey, or of the struggle Luke had to get through near impassable roads. Only when the school grounds were in sight, deep in the heart of a white wilderness of countryside, did Vicky rouse her sister; so Kate was given little opportunity to concoct a plea for leniency on the sixth-former's behalf.

However, she need not have worried. Miss Todd was clearly relieved to have Vicky returned none the worse for her snowy escapade, concerned rather than punitive. St Philippa's, as she reminded them, was a school of Christian foundation and above all wanted its girls to be happy and fulfilled. If the child was not, then it was the fault of the school and not of Victoria. 'One of our most gifted pupils,' she enthused. 'We do not wish Victoria to fall by the wayside.'

Vicky had been swiftly absorbed into a giggling crowd of sixth formers who were hanging over the banisters, desperate for a glimpse of the wondrous Mr Harvey, over whom Vicky had been raving ever since she got back. As they emerged from the head's study it was almost, Kate felt, as if the exploit had been carried out for a dare rather than from any deep-rooted sense of misery. And Vicky's letters told their own tale of restless boredom with school. Now the girl waved them goodbye quite cheerfully, as if the adventure had been fun, but accepting that here was where reality lay. Not for the first time Kate found herself speculating on what Luke could have said to achieve what seemed like a miracle . . .

'Right,' said Luke when they were

back in the car, 'I'm tired, you're tired, it's too late and too dark for us to drive back tonight. I suggest we head for the main road and stop at the first place we come to for a meal and a bed for the night.' He had slung his duffel coat on the back seat while they were in St Philippa's, and his midnight blue suit and the brilliant whiteness of his shirt simply added to that aura of authority and distinction which Kate still found awesome. She had sensed that even Miss Todd, well-used as she must be to highly-educated professional parents, had found the surgeon attractive and imposing.

Vicky's friends had been reduced to gulping shyness.

It suddenly occurred to Kate that, of course, Luke must have come straight from his departmental session. That was why he was dressed so formally. Had he even had time for lunch? How awful of her not to have asked — to have fallen asleep like that, been so inconsiderate. After all, Luke had been up late too, though not, of course, all night.

It was not for her to argue with his plans now, even though she would rather have pressed on so she could get home, somehow, to her father. Of course it was only sensible not to drive into the snowy night in such conditions. All the same, she felt guilty at putting Luke to such inconvenience and expense. Kate bit her lip, knowing there was very little in her purse and not much more in her bank account, even if she had thought to bring her cheque book.

Watching Kate twist her fingers into knots of anxiety, Luke's hand descended comfortingly over hers. 'My treat,' he insisted with a quiet firmness which would brook no argument. 'You remember I threatened we were going to have that talk? Well, now's my chance.'

Kate relaxed into her seat, accepting the inevitable. She wondered if he would bother to ring Dr Crisp and let her know where he was, what excuse he would find to placate her.

'I don't suppose we shall have much difficulty finding an hotel with vacancies,' she ventured. 'There can't be many who would travel far from their homes on a night like this — not if they could help it.'

Luke's concentration was grimly fixed on the white track ahead, illuminated by the car's headlights. It was near impossible to tell where the road began and ended; he must try to follow the compressed tracks of car tyres to avoid ending up in a ditch.

It took them almost an hour to struggle the half-dozen miles to the nearest country inn, a small place with no more than eight rooms but a welcome sight with its snowy, ivy-clad gables, the mullion-paned windows of the dining-room glowing with crimson-shaded lights.

'One double room left, sir,' said the owner with satisfaction, obviously taking them for a thoroughly married couple and respecting Luke's easy air of authority.

'Splendid, splendid,' approved Luke,

rubbing his hands together. 'We have no luggage — came down to visit my niece at St Philippa's and got caught in the snow.' He scrawled rapidly across the open pages of the visitors' book while Kate, knees knocking with mingled embarrassment and confusion, turned aside to hide her scarlet cheeks.

'Ah yes, now if you'll come with me, Mr . . . and Mrs Harvey.' With a broad smile of pleasure the man went before them up a low-beamed staircase hung with gleaming brass and copper pans.

With a reassuring wink, Luke reached for Kate's elbow and drew her to his side. 'Come along, darling,' he urged loudly. 'We'll dine early and then get to bed. You must be exhausted after such a long day.'

'You're not being very funny, Luke,' hissed Kate. '*I'm* not used to this kind of thing even if you are!' She hesitated in the doorway of the bedroom the man was now indicating, immediately aware that it was pretty and cosy and warm, and that under other circumstances the inn would have been a charming place to stay.

'Alone at last!'

Luke hung his coat behind the door and regarded his reluctant companion with a mocking air. He unbuttoned his jacket and draped it across a chair back, pulling off his tie and opening the neck of his shirt.

There was just the one double bed, and not a very large one at that. It might have been a coffin for all the awful fascination it held for Kate. This is my cue to throw a tantrum, she reminded herself. This is the part where in all good books the heroine makes a terrific scene and the man agrees to sleep in the chair with just one blanket, a gentleman to the bitter end.

Out of the corner of her eye she glanced at Luke, who was moving about the room totally unperturbed by the dilemma he knew she must be in. The beast!

With a sinking sensation Kate recalled she had nothing with her, apart from her small clutch bag; nothing to wear in bed, nothing to wash with —

'I haven't even got my toothbrush!' she wailed aloud. 'How can anyone possibly go to bed without cleaning their teeth?'

Luke opened a door on the other side of the room, checking out the bathroom. 'Thinking of bed already?' he grinned. 'Kate Cameron, you've got a one-track mind!'

He got his reward for such levity — a glare that would have stopped a charging rhino. He's waiting for me to tell him he must sleep in that chair, decided Kate. Well, I shan't give him that satisfaction. After all, it's Vicky's fault he's had to drive out here, and but for us Luke would be sleeping in his own bed tonight. Or Harriet's, sneaked a nasty little voice inside, but Kate refused to listen.

No, come what may they would have to share that bed, even if it meant a barrier of pillows down the middle. Otherwise he'd be labelling her the timid little vicar's girl again!

Luke was moving across the room to her now, sliding the red coat from shoulders stiff with tension. 'You can't accuse me of setting you up for this,' he murmured with annoying satisfaction. His breath was warm against the soft skin of her neck as he bent over her, his lips so close to her ear Kate could all but sense his mouth against her flesh . . .

At that moment a tentative knock on the door interrupted them. Swiftly Luke left her side and went to see who was there.

'Our compliments, Mr Harvey, seeing you and your wife were without your things,' came a woman's soft country burr, and with an exclamation of gratitude Luke closed the door on their untimely visitor.

'Good lord, isn't that kind!' He dumped an armful of goodies on to the bedspread. Curiously Kate sorted through the offerings.

'Oh wonderful! Toothbrushes, toothpaste, tissues, shaving tackle for you

— and look at these!' Giggling now at the vision of Luke in plum and red stripes, she held up a thick pair of men's pyjamas, and a passion-killer nightdress which would have swamped even Ethel Lee, back at the hospital.

Luke reached for a tin of talc. 'I'd prefer you in just this,' he leered at her suggestively. 'Chanel No. 5 — mmm.'

'That's terribly expensive,' pointed out Kate sternly. 'I've never used anything except baby powder.'

She was so serious and solemn that Luke covered his smiles with a tactful hand. 'Let's eat soon,' he suggested to his 'bride'. 'You can have the bathroom first.'

Kate skipped happily into the bathroom like a young gazelle. What an adventure! The prospect of a square meal had quite revived her spirits and she would worry about what happened after when the time came. She unfastened the wilting mass of her hair, brushing it into a gleaming silken cape falling way past her waist. Swiftly she darkened her eyelids with subtle bronzey shadow — she still preferred make-up that looked as natural as could be — and stained her full mouth with the cherry gloss Joanna had given her. That would do. She was pale, but ready for anything.

11

Luke chose a quiet corner by the inglenook fireplace and collected their drinks from the bar. Kate couldn't help wondering when he intended to ring Harriet, and said so. 'Shouldn't you ring Dr Crisp and let her know where you are?'

'Why?' asked Luke with a frown.

'Well, since she's come all this way to be with you, I should have thought . . .' The words trailed away as Kate detected a flash of real annoyance ruffle her companion's imperturbability. He appeared to resent her interference so she buried her nose in her sherry glass and tried to ignore her own discomfort.

'I happen to know,' he said icily, 'that Dr Crisp has plans of her own for tonight.'

Fair enough, thought Kate spiritedly; and I hope they include Dr Barnes.

Serve you jolly well right. She immediately felt ashamed of herself, remembering that but for Vicky's escapade they wouldn't be so far from home, and Luke and she would not be spending the evening together either. As for the night, she couldn't bear to consider that far ahead . . .

'Anyway,' continued Luke with that ruthless direct manner that was so unnerving, 'I had the distinct impression you did not much care for Dr Crisp.'

You are a rude man, decided Kate, and not for the first time. The warmth from the fire had brought a glow to her cheeks and her eyes glittered hotly. 'Why on earth should I dislike her? I rather thought it was the other way round.'

'Why should she dislike you?' countered Luke mockingly.

Kate chose to ignore that and gripped her sherry glass so Luke should not see how her fingers trembled with annoyance. One could go off people! Given the rein, Luke was going to ruin what she had hoped would be the most wonderful evening of her life, the two of them alone together at last. She must remind herself to be kind; he'd had a very sad life.

'Dr Barnes told me about your wife,' she said gently. 'I — I saw her photograph that time, in your bedroom. I am so sorry.'

Luke's expression didn't change at all. He continued to regard her levelly. 'I hoped Barnes would put you in the picture. It's not something I care to — '

'Of course not,' Kate interrupted hastily. 'I just felt you should know I had been told.'

Luke nodded and they sat silent for a minute or so before he got up to bring her another sherry. Kate turned towards the hypnotic flickering firelight, thinking of the snow outside and how lovely it was to be there in the cosiness of the inn. She was aware of her companion's return, of the way his penetrating eyes dwelt upon the gleaming sweep of her hair, the transformation of her everyday face into the girl he had seen at the ball. She had always wanted to ask him . . .

'Do you remember where we first met,' she began tentatively, 'that night of the Christmas Ball?'

'How could I forget!' It was a gallant enough response, but the grey eyes were deceptively lazy beneath those drooping speculative lids; his right elbow rested on the damask cloth, lean strong fingers coiled guardedly about his chin as though to conceal from her his expressive humorous mouth, his whole attitude one of conjecture.

'When I saw you that night I took you for a wealthy Californian business-man whose hobby was keeping fit.' Kate giggled at the thought. 'Our doctors tend to look pallid and care-worn, don't you think? As if they could use a good meal and a decent night's sleep.'

Luke grimaced good-humouredly. 'My dear Kate, at the moment, though I may not look it, I could use both of those things. Still, I take your comment as a compliment — whether it was meant that way or not!'

Emboldened by two glasses of sherry on an empty stomach, Kate reached out and put her hand kindly over his, giving it a little shake to support her words. 'Of course! I mean to say you looked absolutely marvellous — so tanned and strong and . . . and rugged. Everyone was positively swooning. Didn't you notice the silly things?'

Luke was grinning openly now. 'How could I, when I only had eyes for you? And you looked far too assured and sophisticated to be caught swooning over anyone.'

Kate blushed and avoided those mocking, dangerous eyes. 'You're teasing me,' she accused. 'But I do happen to think it's a bit pathetic the way a lot of the staff carry on, having affairs that mean nothing to either side. I'm not that sort of person, as you may already have noticed.'

'It's possible to go too far in the opposite direction though, Kate.' Luke paused for a moment as if to assess the effect of his words, studying the delicate profile turned now towards the fire. 'Or perhaps you find doctors particularly intimidating.'

Kate froze with alarm. What had caused such a turn in the conversation? For a long moment she truly hated Luke as he sat there, analysing her with such probing calm. It was as if he could see right into her head and found what he saw there peculiarly fascinating.

Sensing that she was poised for flight, Luke made every effort now to be charming. He led her into the low-ceilinged candle-lit dining-room, chatted about life at the hospital, inconsequential small talk while a waitress set before them a whole tureen of steaming vegetable soup.

'So,' drawled Luke, ladling a generous helping into Kate's soup bowl, 'you thought I must be some rich playboy, eh? It must have been one hell of a shock when I turned up as part of Miss Westropp's inquisition.'

Kate's spoon wobbled unsteadily as she raised it to her lips. 'You didn't even recognise me!' As she spoke she discovered a strong impulse to challenge him.

Luke chuckled over his soup. 'Lady, I knew who you were the moment you walked through that door. Cinderella, after the ball was over.'

'If you were the Prince, I thought you distinctly *uncharming*! That parting shot about my beanpole height . . . '

'Did I really say that?' Luke looked more amused than ashamed of himself. 'I guessed you were one of the nursing staff. Those chapped little paws gave the game away — even though the rest of you looked like someone David Bailey photographs for a living.'

Kate sighed ecstatically, longing to pinch herself to find out if she was really awake or dreaming. Luke Harvey sitting there opposite, saying the sort of things he only said in her wildest dreams . . .

'I remember how surprised I was when you did speak,' she recalled, spreading her brown roll with a dollop of butter. 'No Yankee accent after all, just good old BBC English.'

'Well, I did go to Winchester,' mumbled Luke through a mouthful of crumbs. 'And I read Psychology and Physiology up at Oxford before studying clinical medicine proper. It has always fascinated me, the way the human mind works.'

Oh-oh, no wonder he handled Vicky so well. 'I'm truly grateful to you, Luke, for the way you got my sister to return to school. What ever did you say to her?'

Luke tapped the side of his nose mysteriously. 'That's between me and Vicky. Seriously though, I am very interested in counselling. Your sister wanted to prove to herself she wasn't forgotten, that you still cared enough to call a halt to her messing about. It made her feel loved and safe. And she's not really unhappy at school as you saw, just a little bored and looking for a way to stir things up a bit.'

'Yes, I do see that. Basically Vicky is a dear. It's just lately she's been — well, rather awkward.'

'I find it fascinating, the likeness between the two of you,' mused Luke. 'Vicky is you — with everything more intense. You painted in vivid colours.'

That's me, thought Kate bitterly. Dull *brown* Kate — safe and boring.

'You seem to be hitting it off with Hayden Barnes,' Luke continued unexpectedly, helping himself to yet more of the delicious soup. 'After such an unfortunate start.'

'Actually,' said Kate on an impulse, 'we're thinking of getting engaged.' God forgive her the lie; but it wouldn't hurt to let Luke Harvey think *some-body* found her exciting enough to fall in love with.

His spoon half-way to his mouth, Luke stopped eating and stared at her. Kate didn't know what reaction she had expected from him, though blatant jealousy would have been wonderful to behold.

'Really?' he said with wary surprise — almost, Kate felt, as though he knew something she did not, and felt sorry for her because of it.

Then, as if the topic of her love-life were of little interest, he turned the conversation back to himself.

'That night of the ball,' he was telling her now, 'I thought in my cynical fashion that if I let you open your mouth my ears would be assailed by the sort of dreadful accent most fashion models seem to affect these days. There couldn't be much of a brain behind so beautiful a face and body ... I just wanted to enjoy looking at you, holding you in my arms.'

'Crumbs!' gasped Kate, astonished into inelegance by this unexpected turn of events but refusing to allow herself to be overwhelmed by clever-sounding phrases. 'I'd love to believe you Luke Harvey, but unfortunately I think you're just trying to subdue me by flattery.'

'And to think I suspected I was boring you to distraction!'

All the same, she bent flaming cheeks over her plate, feigning enormous fascination with the tenderest of fillet steaks.

Luke called for another bottle of that rich and heady red wine. 'I realise now,' he was telling her very seriously, all mockery gone from his sombre tone, 'that when you saw Lydia's photograph by my bed you drew your own conclusions. I have since tried to speak to you alone, to explain, but you went out of your way to elude me . . .'

This was hardly the moment to let him know she had thought he was out to ruin her career. Or that she had poked her nose into Lydia's bedroom-shrine. She just said simply, 'I'm very sorry about that and I hope you can forgive me.' So much more was becoming clear — the resemblance between herself and Luke's dead wife; his anxiety lest Maurice Hall discover her presence in his home, and be hurt by it . . .

'Why did you decide to come back to England?' she asked dazedly. 'Was it because of Professor Hall?'

Luke sighed and drank a long draught of wine. 'Someone I had to escape from,' he muttered beneath his breath.

Kate looked puzzled. What on earth could he mean? 'I beg your pardon?' she queried, but Luke shook his head as if regretting his words already.

'We will always be close, my father-in-law and I. I could do nothing that would cause him pain. You know, I was so proud to be his clinical assistant. That's why I'm so enjoying this post, testing out the limits of my surgical skills. If I can progress to a consultancy — well, I must just see how things work out. If not,' he shrugged, 'I could do far worse than go back to a country where there's a crying need for medical help.'

'Yet here you are,' Kate reminded him softly. 'What brought you home, Luke? Tell me, I want to know all there is to know about you.'

If she could have bitten off her tongue she would have at that moment. A warning flash of intuition cried, 'Stop!' But it was too late.

Luke was alert now, snapping out of

his reverie. His eyes upon her were cruel, hurtful, seeking to wound. 'So you want to know all about me, do you? You might as well.

'I had a very stormy affair with Harriet after her husband was killed. Yes, I thought that would repulse you . . . Mutual consolation, you might call it. But I came back here to escape her. And what happens? She follows me — says she plans to stay. I see you gasp, and well you may, because, my dear girl, do you know where Harriet is tonight? She's with your lover, Hayden Barnes!'

It was Luke's turn to look shattered when, far from fainting with horror, Kate burst into laughter, causing the other diners to turn and smile approvingly and raise their glasses to the couple.

'Hayden's not my lover,' she spluttered mirthfully. 'I only told you we were getting engaged to make you jealous. To be honest, Luke, I was hoping she would fall for Hayden and leave you sad and lonely so I could make you better. And I could if you would only give me a chance.'

Luke had a table napkin pressed hard to his lips. For once he seemed totally at a loss for words. 'Come upstairs with me, young lady. There's something I've been longing to give you for ages,' he managed at long last.

'Oh no,' teased Kate, suddenly and wonderfully sure of herself. 'We stay here and finish our meal. I can't resist the sweet-trolley — and do you know, I think I could manage a brandy tonight.'

'And so could I,' murmured Luke, his eyes devouring her. 'And so could I.'

12

Kate awoke next morning to the clink of teacups and a maid drawing back floral chintz curtains to reveal a clear and ice-blue sky. At first she could not recall what had brought her to this unfamiliar room. Her aching head was being pounded by some unrelenting sledge-hammer and even the thin wintry light felt cruelly harsh to her sensitive eyes.

The girl brought over the tea-tray and placed it on the night table on Kate's side of the double bed, then with a shy smile left the room. Propping herself on her elbows, Kate surveyed her surroundings, a frown of perplexity creasing her smooth brow. Something had happened the night before — something pretty amazing, though the details danced in her brain in a teasing welter of confusion . . .

At that moment a half-naked man came striding from the adjacent bathroom, whistling tunelessly, freshly-shampooed hair rubbed into damp feathery curls, a decidedly small towel hitched about his middle region. Sinewy muscles rippled beneath smooth brown skin and not an ounce of spare flesh marred the superbly powerful frame paused now at the foot of the bed and saying something — Kate wasn't sure what — as her throat went dry and she slunk further into the safety of the bed.

'What?' Inwardly she cursed the insistent thumping going on inside her skull, shrinking beneath the scrutiny of a triumphantly grinning Luke Harvey. He looked more satisfied with himself than ever!

'I asked you if you always snore,' he repeated pleasantly enough, arms akimbo, amused by such obvious discomfiture.

'I *never* snore!' Indignant eyes flashed warily above sheets pulled tightly up to the delicate pointed chin.

'How would you know?' he pointed

out in tones of such infuriating reasonableness that Kate found herself grinding her teeth helplessly. 'You were sound asleep. Kept *me* awake for hours.'

'Well you don't look too bad on it,' muttered his victim. 'Ooh, my poor head.' With a groan Kate closed her eyes and let her head sink back into the downy comfort of the pillows.

Luke crossed to the wardrobe, delved into the jacket of his suit and came back with a clear plastic phial. 'Swallow a couple of these — they're magic.' He dropped down beside her on the bed, efficiently organised two strong cups of tea, slipped two pills into Kate's open palm and downed two himself with a good gulp of the steaming brew.

Kate looked doubtfully at her companion and then at the obvious hollow in the pillow next to hers, the crumpled sheets and blankets. She was actually wearing that monstrous nightdress! And her own clothes had been slung far from neatly across a nearby chair . . .

Had he? Or hadn't he? And how did one ask? Or, if she hadn't really and truly dreamed it all, was it all that important if he . . . ?

Luke was lounging happily across her legs, looking more relaxed and carefree than she could ever remember seeing him before. Kate's heart began to swell with pride and love and tenderness. But all the same, she still could not be sure.

She managed a convincing glower from underneath the frowning arch of her eyebrows. 'I want to know exactly what happened last night,' she told the surgeon sternly, preferring to hear it all from his own lips than to trust to her over-heated imagination.

But Luke was in no mood to be merciful. 'To the astonishment of all and sundry, you leapt to your feet in the dining-room, shrieked, 'At last — I'm engaged!', then passed out like a light on the carpet at your husband's feet.'

'Rubbish!' snorted Kate, almost choking on her tea. 'I do recall getting to the door of this room before I flaked out.

You ought to be ashamed of yourself, you must have known I wasn't used to all that wine!' She shook her head dazedly, 'But after that I can't remember a thing — '

'Well, allow me to fill in the gaps,' related Luke with exaggerated relish. 'First I undressed you, then I put you to bed.'

'Oh no!' Overcome with mortification, Kate buried her head in her hands, refusing to meet the mocking grey eyes which sought to trap her own in their unfathomable depths.

'Don't fret yourself,' advised Luke kindly. 'You know how we professionals feel about bodies — totally impervious. And after all, you did agree I could make an honest woman of you — or perhaps you don't remember that either? Well now, I'm sure I told you I had something to give you.'

Once more he dug deep into his jacket pocket and came up this time with a round blue jeweller's box. 'It's a Victorian one,' he explained. 'When I saw this in a shop in Cambridge I realised it was perfect — just as pretty and old-fashioned as you.'

Kate caught her breath in wonderment as on to the third finger of her left hand — the miracle come true! — Luke slid the most enchanting ring; a glowing-bright emerald encircled in a delicate filigree of gold and pearls. 'There — your fingers are so slender I shall have to get it made a little smaller. D'you realise I've been carrying this around for weeks, ever since I made my mind up?' He sounded just as happy and excited as a schoolboy, and Kate's incredulous leaping joy overflowed all bounds of propriety. She flung herself out of the bedclothes and into Luke's arms so violently they both gasped at the impact.

And later, when they could bring themselves to break apart for a few seconds, the questions came tumbling from lips still throbbing from his ardent kisses. 'Oh, Luke, my darling, to think I believed you were spying on me because of that row with Hayden

Barnes. Can it be true you wanted just to see *me*?'

'Well,' said Luke modestly, stroking her hair, 'I had certainly picked you out as the hot favourite: But I admit I was testing you out in my fashion.' He looked suddenly so solemn that Kate drew back from his embrace, the laughter fading slowly from her eyes.

'I don't understand . . . '

'I had it in my mind to return one day to Africa. If you came with me you would need to be tough, resilient and capable. But it didn't take me long to discover that in spite of your Dresden looks you were all of those things.'

Equally solemn glowing eyes looked trustingly into his. 'Is that what you want, my darling? To go back to the mission hospital? Because you know I'll follow you to the ends of the earth. Though,' she added practical as ever, 'I must finish my training first.'

Luke shook his head, unsure even now in his own heart. 'It saddens me to know Harriet has abandoned our hospital. But I'm thirty-five and I want a family of my own, born here in my own country. And you, Kate, you're still so young — can you really want to tie yourself down to an arrogant, ageing surgeon?'

'I'm a grown woman, Luke! And please don't forget I'm almost twenty-one — '

Kate's proud words brought a rueful smile to Luke's face. 'I dare not imagine what your father's reaction will be. Is he as prejudiced as you were against the medical profession?'

Kate shook her head violently, colouring as she did so. 'Of course he isn't! And as for me . . . ' If ever she had mistrusted the doctors she had worked with, or rather her own ability to relax and enjoy their company, then she preferred to forget such foolishness. There had been such a deal of growing up over the past few months.

With a start she realised that Luke was regarding her with the utmost tenderness and pride, as if he could not tear his gaze from the gravity of her face. 'Luke,' she began hesitantly, afraid to put it into words yet knowing that she must, 'do I make you think of Lydia?' The warm, painful heat stole over her neck and cheeks as though his reply might prove unbearable.

Once again he seemed to know and understand her thoughts and fears in that uncanny way of his. 'You goose,' he whispered, gathering her close against him, his strong arms so safe and comforting even through the thick folds of flannelette enclosing her trembling body.

'I admit I picked you out of that gaggle of females because you looked rather like Lydia — tall and dark with that cloud of wonderful hair billowing over your shoulders — but I never see the likeness now. Your personality is so utterly different. Lydia was something of a spoiled darling — she had everything she ever wanted, including me. No, I could no more confuse the two of you than I could confuse you and your sister, young Vicky!'

Relief washed over Kate, convinced as never before that their love was meant to be. She managed a spluttery giggle through the tears that had spilled over from her troubled eyes. 'Do you know, I thought it was probably because I towered over all the other girls in those ridiculous shoes I was wearing!'

'Come to think of it, you certainly did! Hey now, what do you say we get dressed and breakfasted and on our way?'

Kate marvelled at how easy and natural it was to grab hold of that strong masculine wrist and check the time on Luke's gold wrist-watch. 'I wish you didn't have that long drive back to Stambridge — the roads are so bad.'

'We're not going back to Stambridge — I'm taking you home. This has got to be done properly you know. I'm going down on bended knees to beg for your hand in marriage.'

'Luke, you can't!' Not for nothing was there a practical head on Kate's shoulders. 'You'd never get back in time for your lecture to the medical students tomorrow. Just drop me at my flat and I'll go on ahead by train until you can join us at the vicarage.'

'Hark to the voice of reason. All right, all right.' A reluctant grimace distorted the beloved features of her fiancé. 'But hear this, my girl. I forbid you to break the news until I get there. I want this to be a surprise to your family.'

'Oh it'll be that all right, I promise you. Probably send Dad into cardiac arrest . . . No, no, silly!' at the look of dismay on Luke's face, 'I'm only joking, he's really fit as a flea. I promise, we'll do it your way.'

* * *

Alice had cooked them all a wonderful supper of jugged hare.

'Delicious, my dear,' exclaimed Michael

Cameron, dabbing the corners of his mouth with a napkin. 'We haven't had jugged hare for years, have we, Kate?'

'And it tasted just as good as Mother's,' insisted Kate generously, paying Alice the highest compliment she could think of. All the same, it did give one an odd sensation to watch another woman take charge in the kitchen which had once been the territory of her tall dark mother.

She had been home now for two whole days — and there was scarcely anything Alice would allow her to do. It was kindly meant, but the enforced idleness only allowed Kate more time to brood upon the fact that there had been no word from Luke, not even the briefest phone call. She found herself wondering about him constantly. When would he come? Could he possibly have had a change of heart about her?

'You enjoy a bit of rest, my pet,' insisted Alice maternally. 'The Lord knows you nurses work your fingers to the bone. Just sit there by the fire in the rocking-chair, enjoy your coffee and tell me all about the hospital life. I love to hear you chat away while I get on with baking bread and pies. It's good for me to keep occupied, now my boys are away at school and college.'

So Kate sat and watched and speculated about her father and about Alice Rayner. Though her hair was prematurely grey, Alice's face was soft and unlined with neat, gentle features. She could be no more than forty-five. Just ten years older than Luke.

Late that afternoon Kate was inveigled into the study for a private chat. Michael and Alice wished to marry, she must be the first to know; it was only to be with the approval of both their families. Impetuously Kate hugged her father and assured him of his daughters' delighted support, and of their relief to know he would be loved and cared for by someone as warm and generous-hearted as Alice.

'And Vicky and I will have three new step-brothers. I bet she'll be over the moon, having them here with her in the holidays. I take it that will be the arrangement?'

Michael Cameron grinned and nodded. 'They're grand chaps, Kate. Bring the vicarage to life a bit, won't they?'

'Dad, it couldn't be more splendid! Now, if you don't need me for anything I think I shall go into church and polish up the 'Wedding March'.'

It was with a special secret glow that Kate left the study and disappeared upstairs to her own bedroom. There she pulled on her thickest tights and a short tweed skirt, topping the lot with two pullovers. It was cold in the unheated church when there was not a service; freezing up there in the organ loft. Her face was scrubbed and clean, for back home was no place for the sophisticated tricks Joanna had taught her, and her hair swung Cinderella-style in a heavy plait which dangled over her right shoulder, almost to her narrow waist.

Alone in the darkened church, Kate turned on the light above the organ and threw the switch which sent the motor humming into action.

Absorbed in the music she was making, Kate played on for ages, forgetful even of the cold; a tiny figure high over the chancel, hidden by green curtains and dwarfed by the great pan-pipes rearing overhead.

When the agitated figure of the vicar materialised at her elbow Kate stopped abruptly in mid-chord, the Mendelssohn coming to an untimely end. 'Dad! Whatever is the matter?'

For an answer her father jerked aside the curtain so that it slid away on a rattle of brass rings. He pointed a shaking finger down towards a shadowy figure standing there in the main aisle.

'That young man has asked my permission to marry you, Kate! He tells me he is a surgeon from the hospital and his name is — '

'Darling!' called Kate, her heart swelling huge with joy and pride. For down there in the gloom, head thrown back, stood Luke, eyes fixed upon Kate in the centre of that pool of golden light. She saw him raise his hand to his lips, blow a silent kiss towards her. With answering fingers she returned that kiss and sent it floating back. To Luke Harvey, her Prince most Charming, her one and only love.

DARK SUSPICION

Susan Udy

When Aunt Jessica asks Caitlin to help run her art gallery while she is in hospital, Caitlin agrees. She hadn't bargained on having to deal with a series of thefts, however — or Jessica's insistence that Caitlin's new employer, Nicholas Millward, must be responsible. Nicholas is as ruthless as he is handsome, but would he really stoop to theft? And what can Caitlin do when she finds herself in the grip of a passion too powerful to resist?

HER SEARCHING HEART

Phyllis Mallet

A proposal of marriage from Robert, whom she does not love, brings Valerie face to face with a frightening question — is she incapable of falling in love? She rejects Robert and flees to the tranquility of Cornwall, hoping to find the answer; but when she meets Bruce and his motherless young daughter Mandy, she discovers new and disturbing emotions deep in her heart — and finds the answer to her question . . .

HEAD OVER HEELS

Cindy Procter-King

Magee Sinclair keeps making costly blunders at her family's advertising agency, so when handsome Justin Kane, head of CycleMania, needs her to pose as his girlfriend for the weekend in exchange for a lucrative campaign, she has little choice but to say yes. Justin needs to cement a deal with Willoughby Bikes by impressing the Willoughbys while they bike trails together. But Magee has landed herself in major trouble — she doesn't know one end of a mountain bike from the other . . .

BACHELOR BID

Sarah Evans

City slicker Benedict Laverton is billed as top prize at the Coolumbarup Bachelors' Ball. To escape the ordeal, he persuades one of the organizers, Rosy Scott, into bidding for him with his own money. But Rosy gets carried away, bidding a cool $10,000 . . . When she goes on stage to claim her man, Rosy not only has to face Benedict's stunned disbelief, she has to kiss him too — a kiss which is spectacular enough to convince her that getting involved with Benedict will end in disaster . . .

SECRET SANTA

Anne Ryan

Jade is a journalist, attached to her boyfriend, Brad, but impossibly drawn to photographer Carl. With Christmas approaching, an exotic Secret Santa gift at work confuses her further, but why does Carl run a mile whenever the heat starts to sizzle between them? Family problems add to Jade's seasonal blues — can she find contentment before the big day arrives . . . ?